JAKE M

GRAPHIC

TRUST ON THIN ICE

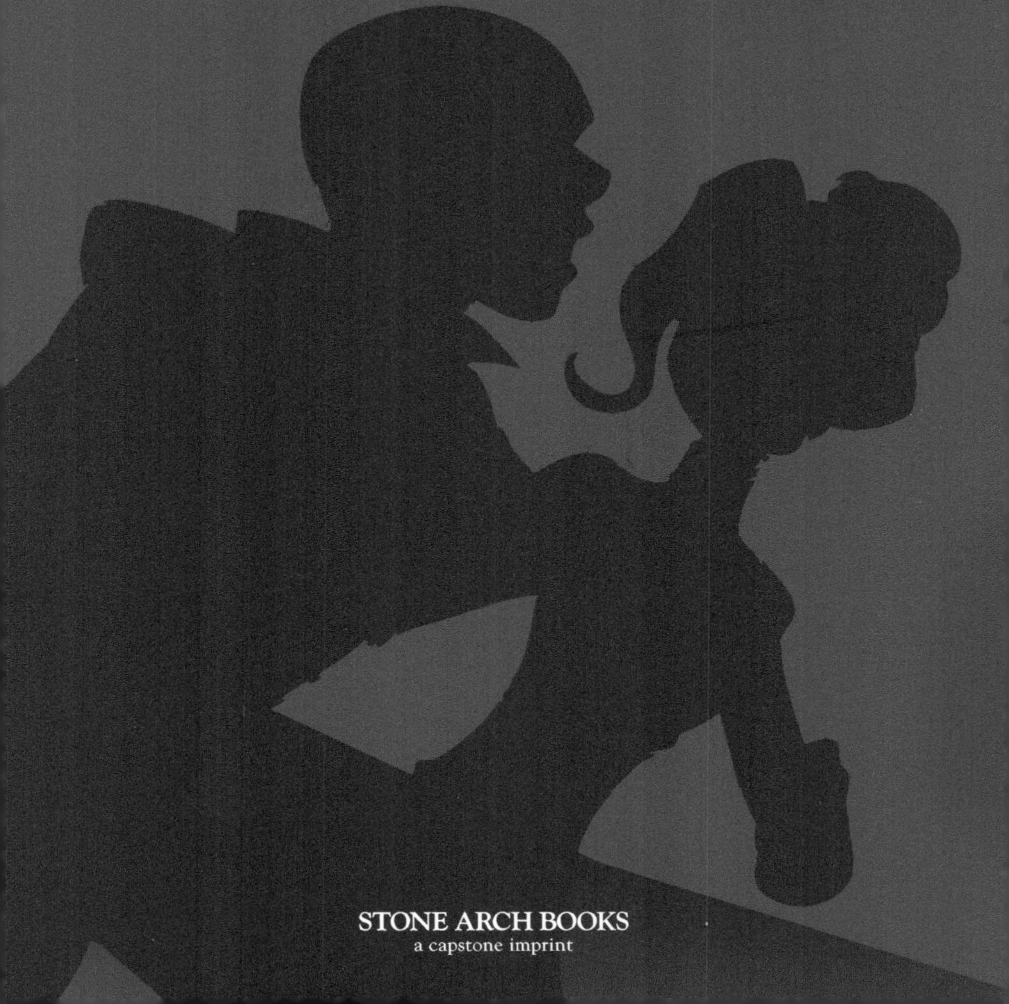

STONE ARCH BOOKS
a capstone imprint

JAKE MADDOX
GRAPHIC NOVELS

Published by Stone Arch Books,
an imprint of Capstone.
1710 Roe Crest Drive
North Mankato, Minnesota 56003
capstonepub.com

Library of Congress Cataloging-in-Publication Data
Names: Maddox, Jake, author. | Alves, Lelo, illustrator. |
Muñiz, Berenice, cover artist.
Title: Trust on thin ice / by Jake Maddox ; illustrated by
Lelo Alves ; cover art by Berenice Muniz.
Description: North Mankato, Minnesota : Stone Arch
Books, [2023] | Series: Jake Maddox graphic novels |
Audience: Ages 8-12 | Audience: Grades 4-6 | Summary:
Mina is a talented figure skater who is looking forward
to trying the new challenge of pairs skating, but with shy
boy Luke, she is beginning to have second thoughts, so
they will have to overcome their trust issues to become a
successful team.
Identifiers: LCCN 2022029339 (print) | LCCN 2022029340
(ebook) | ISBN 9781666341423 (hardcover) | ISBN
9781666341461 (paperback) | ISBN 9781666341478 (pdf) |
ISBN 9781666341492 (kindle edition)
Subjects: CYAC: Graphic novels. | Ice skating—Fiction. |
Trust—Fiction. | Teamwork (Sports)—Fiction. | LCGFT:
Sports comics. | Graphic novels.
Classification: LCC PZ7.7.M332 Tt 2023 (print) |
LCC PZ7.7.M332 (ebook) | DDC 741.5/973—dc23/
eng/20220812
LC record available at https://lccn.loc.gov/2022029339
LC ebook record available at https://lccn.loc.
gov/2022029340

Editor: Amanda Robbins
Designer: Heidi Thompson
Production Specialist: Tori Abraham

Printed in the United States   5953

TRUST ON THIN ICE

Text by Katie Schenkel
Art by Lelo Alves
Cover Art by Berenice Muñiz

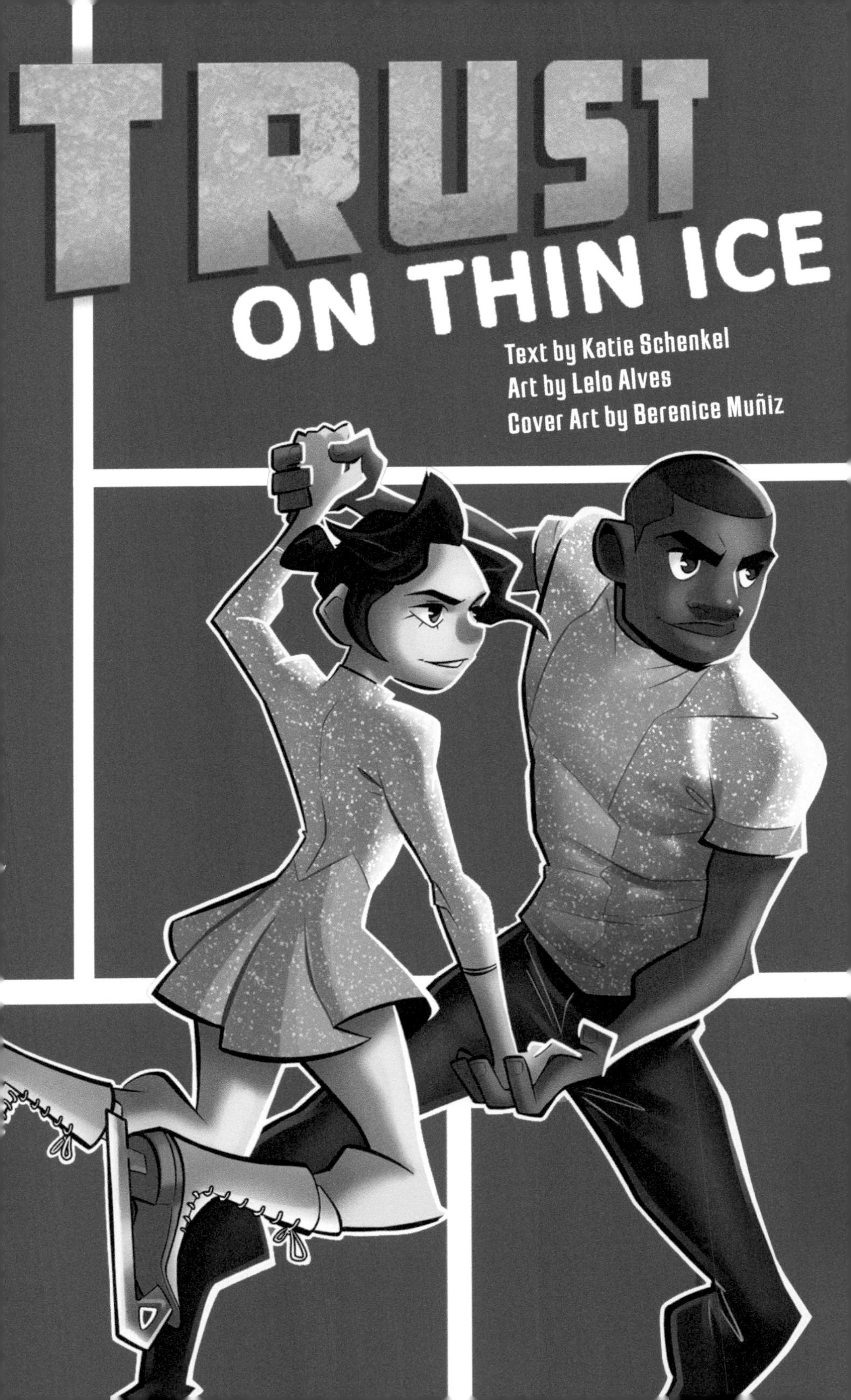

CAST OF CHARACTERS

Mina Kee **Luke Davis**

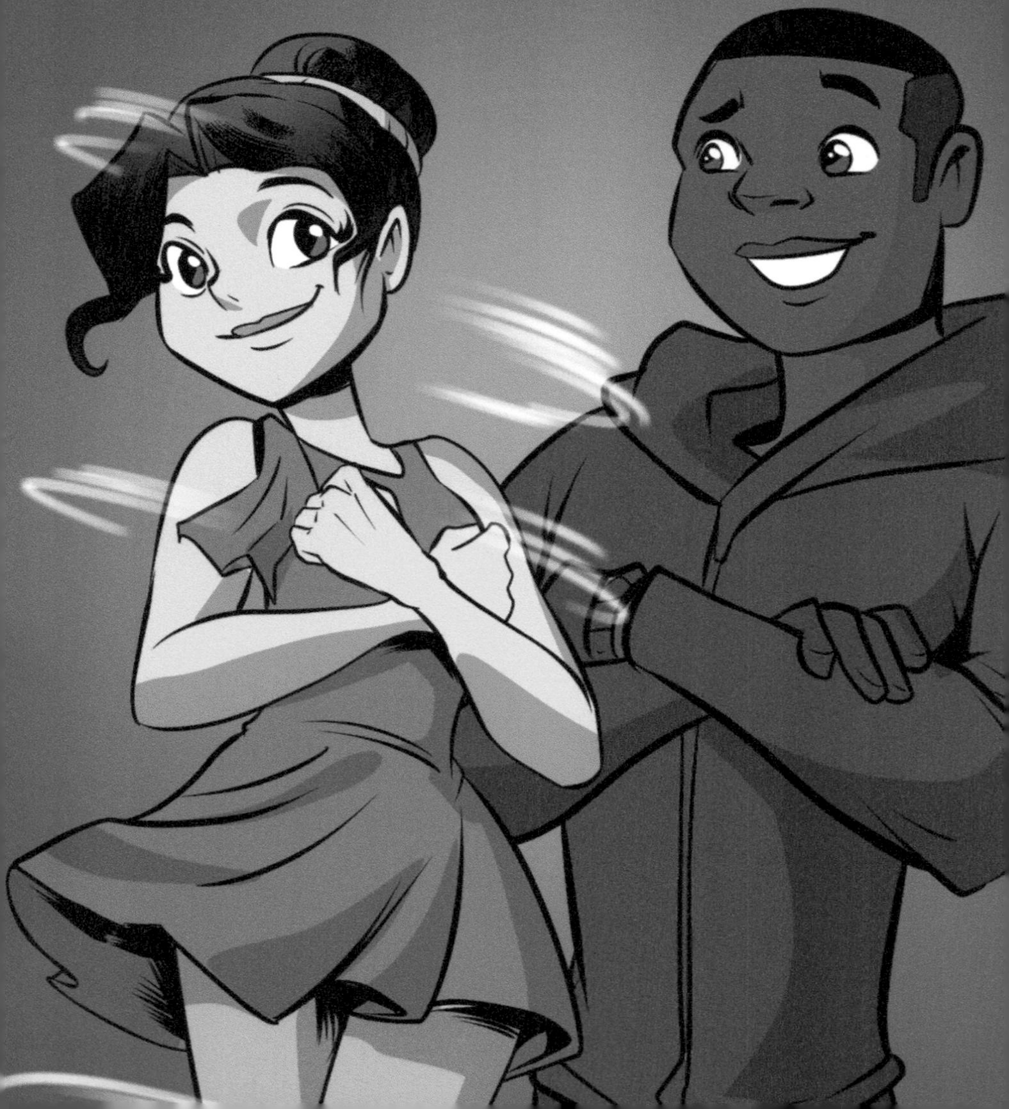

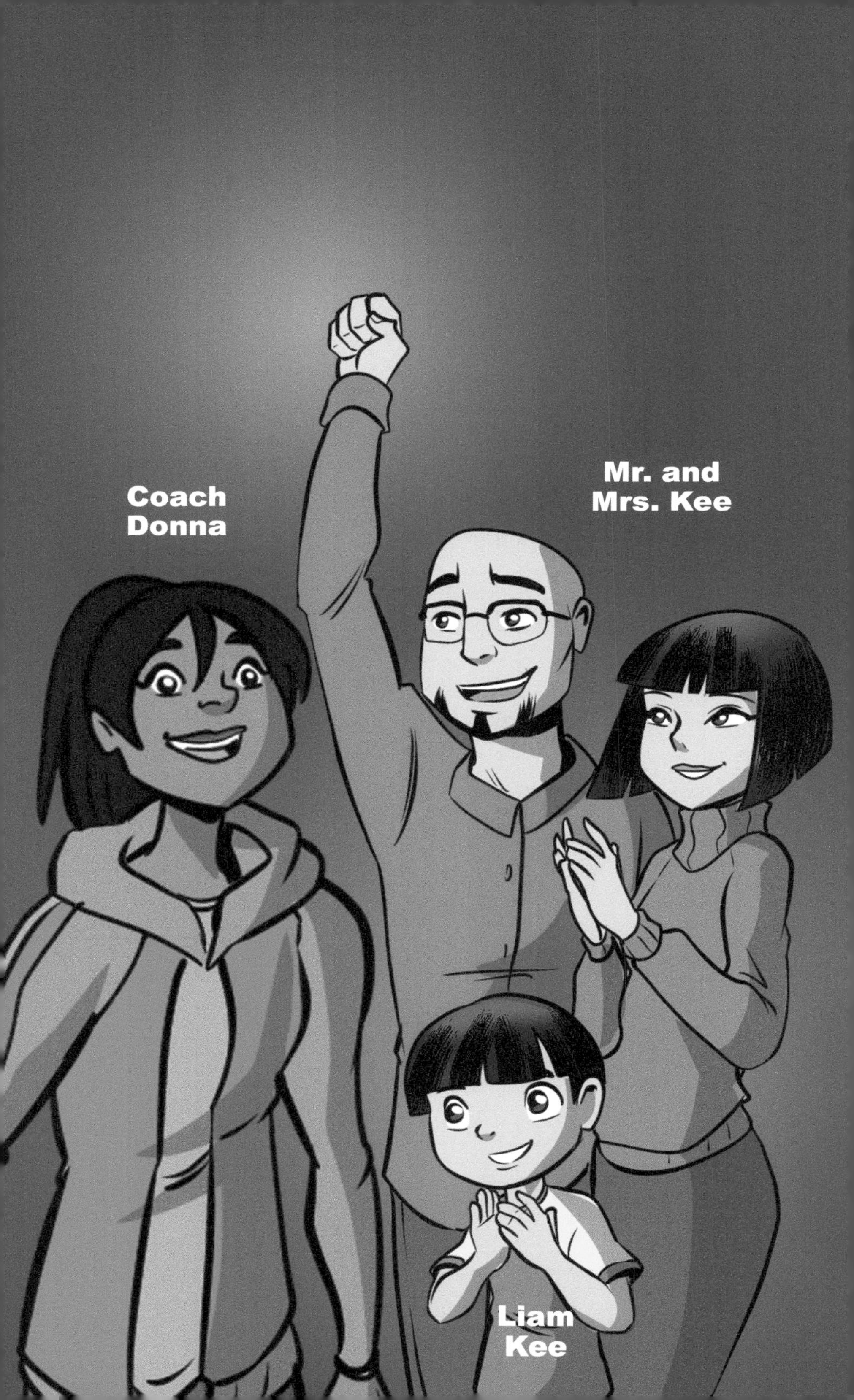
Coach
Donna
Mr. and
Mrs. Kee
Liam
Kee

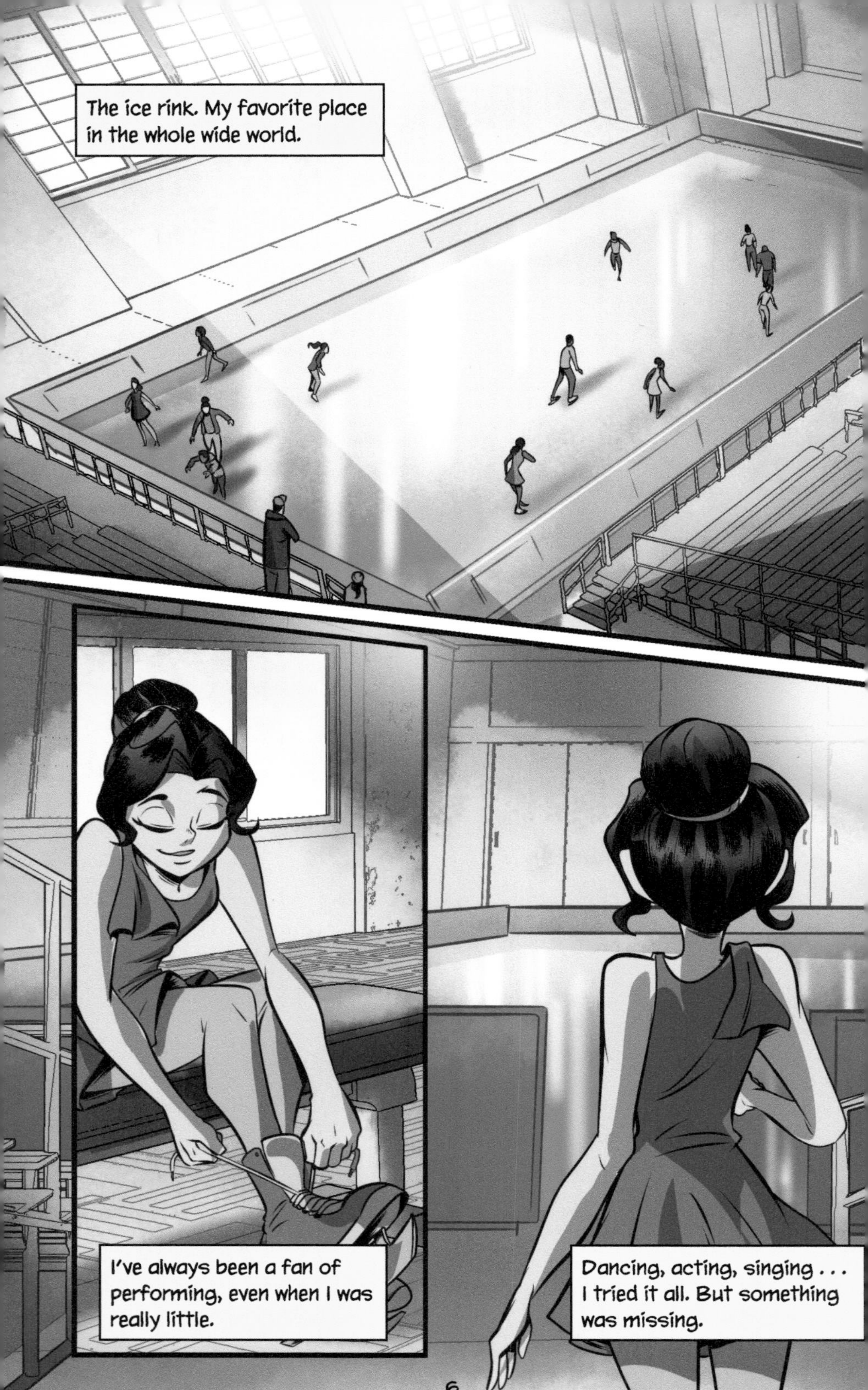
The ice rink. My favorite place in the whole wide world.
I've always been a fan of performing, even when I was really little.
Dancing, acting, singing . . . I tried it all. But something was missing.

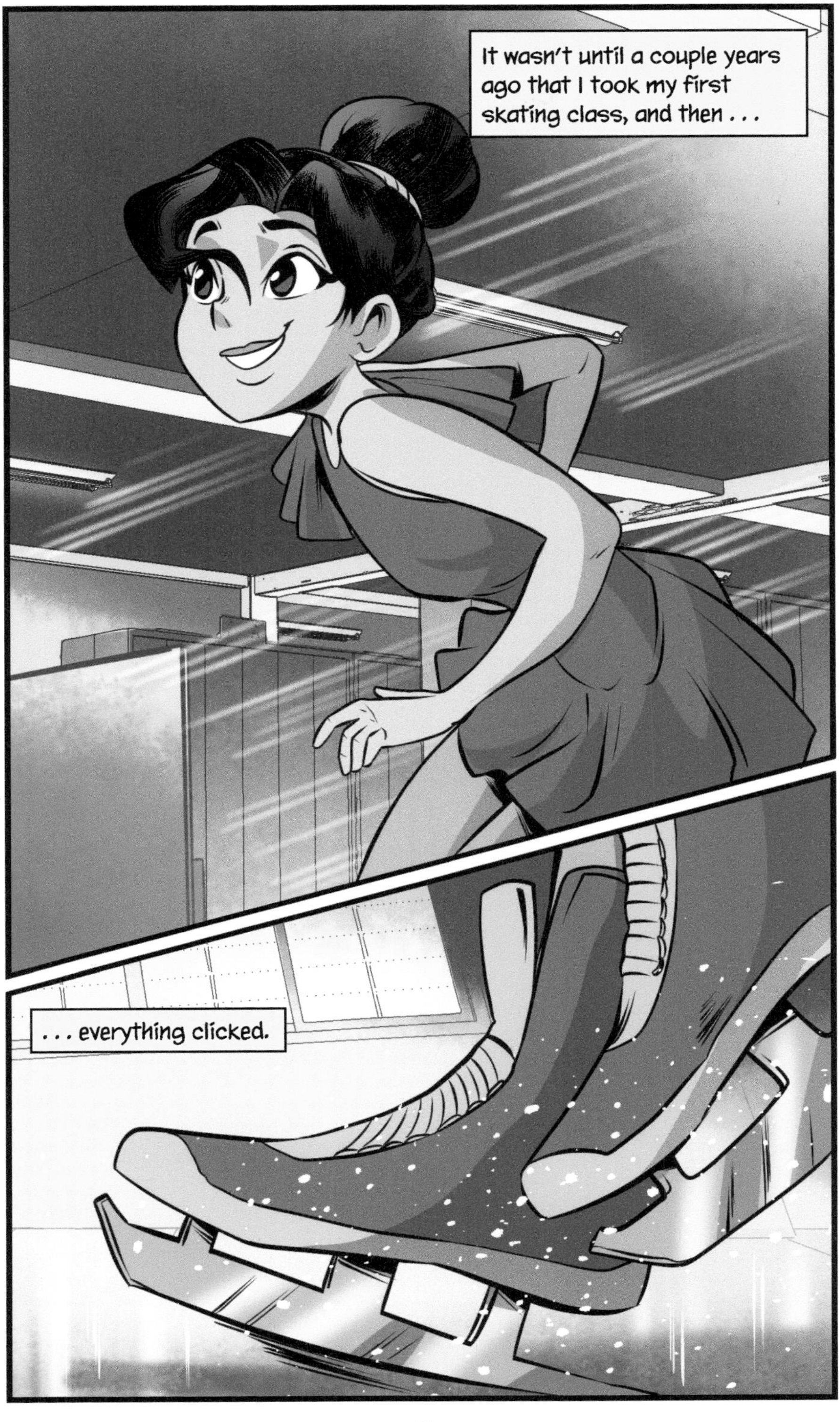
It wasn't until a couple years ago that I took my first skating class, and then . . .
. . . everything clicked.

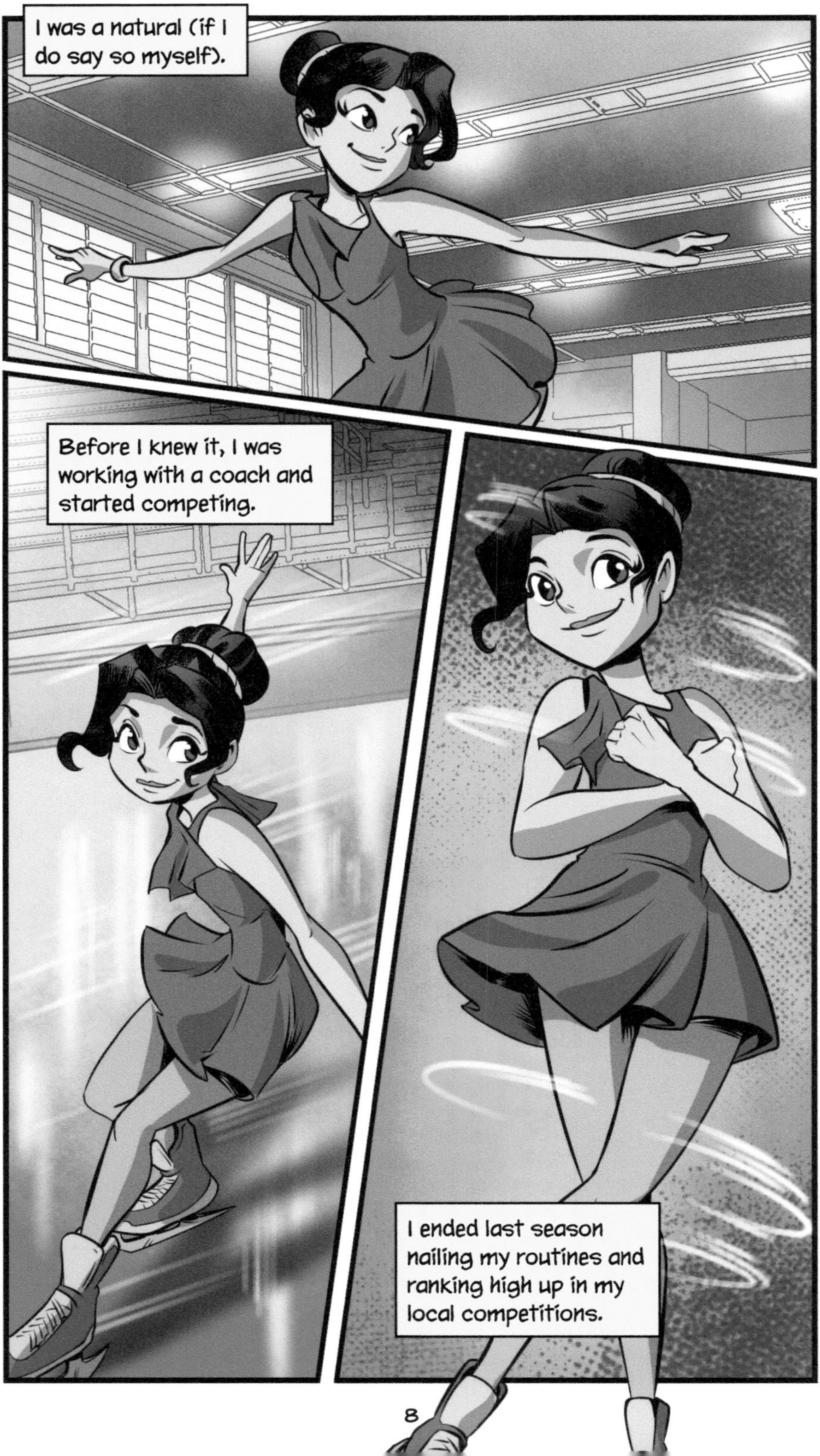
I was a natural (if I do say so myself).
Before I knew it, I was working with a coach and started competing.
I ended last season nailing my routines and ranking high up in my local competitions.

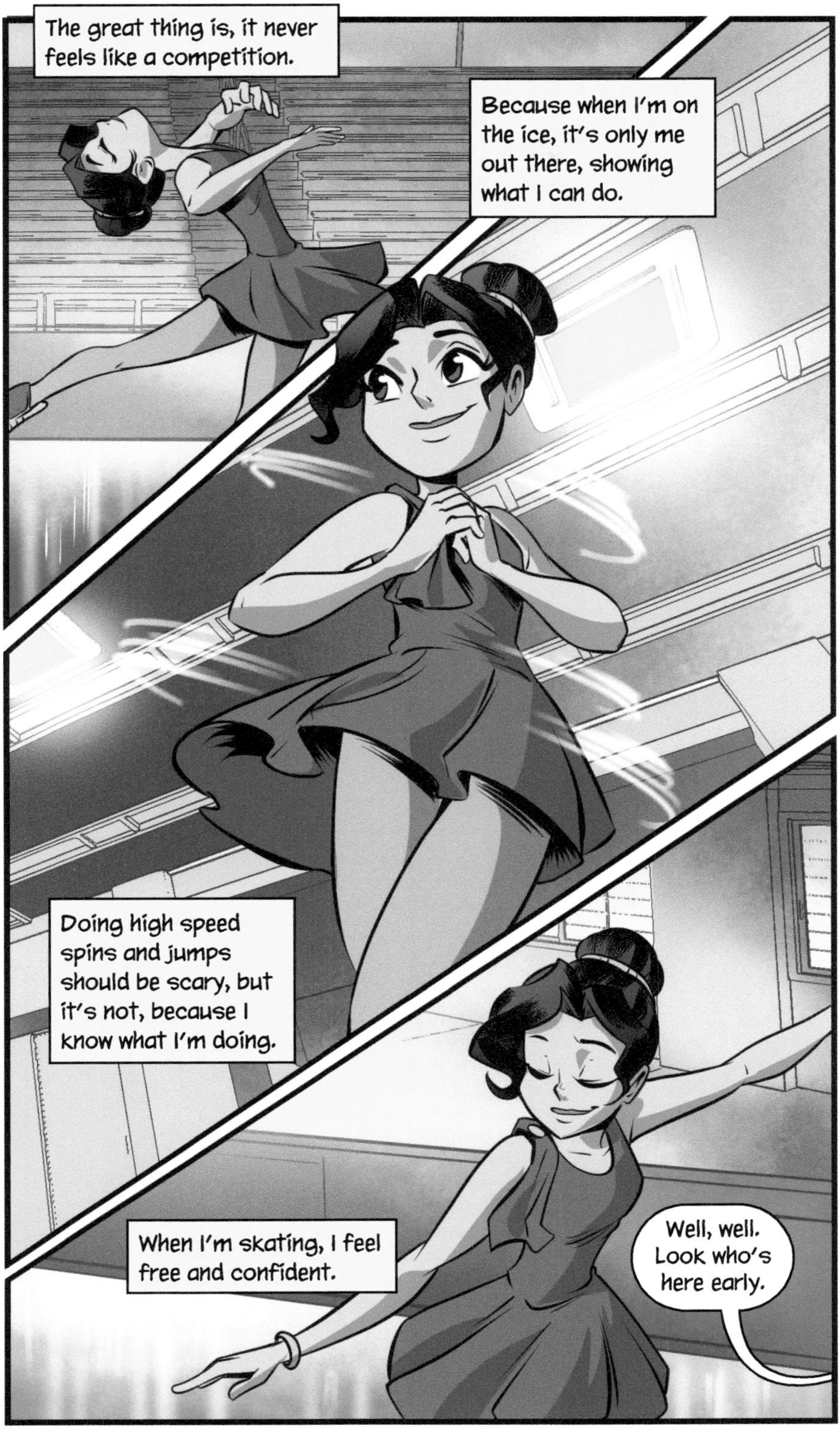
The great thing is, it never feels like a competition.
Because when I'm on the ice, it's only me out there, showing what I can do.
Doing high speed spins and jumps should be scary, but it's not, because I know what I'm doing.
When I'm skating, I feel free and confident.
Well, well. Look who's here early.

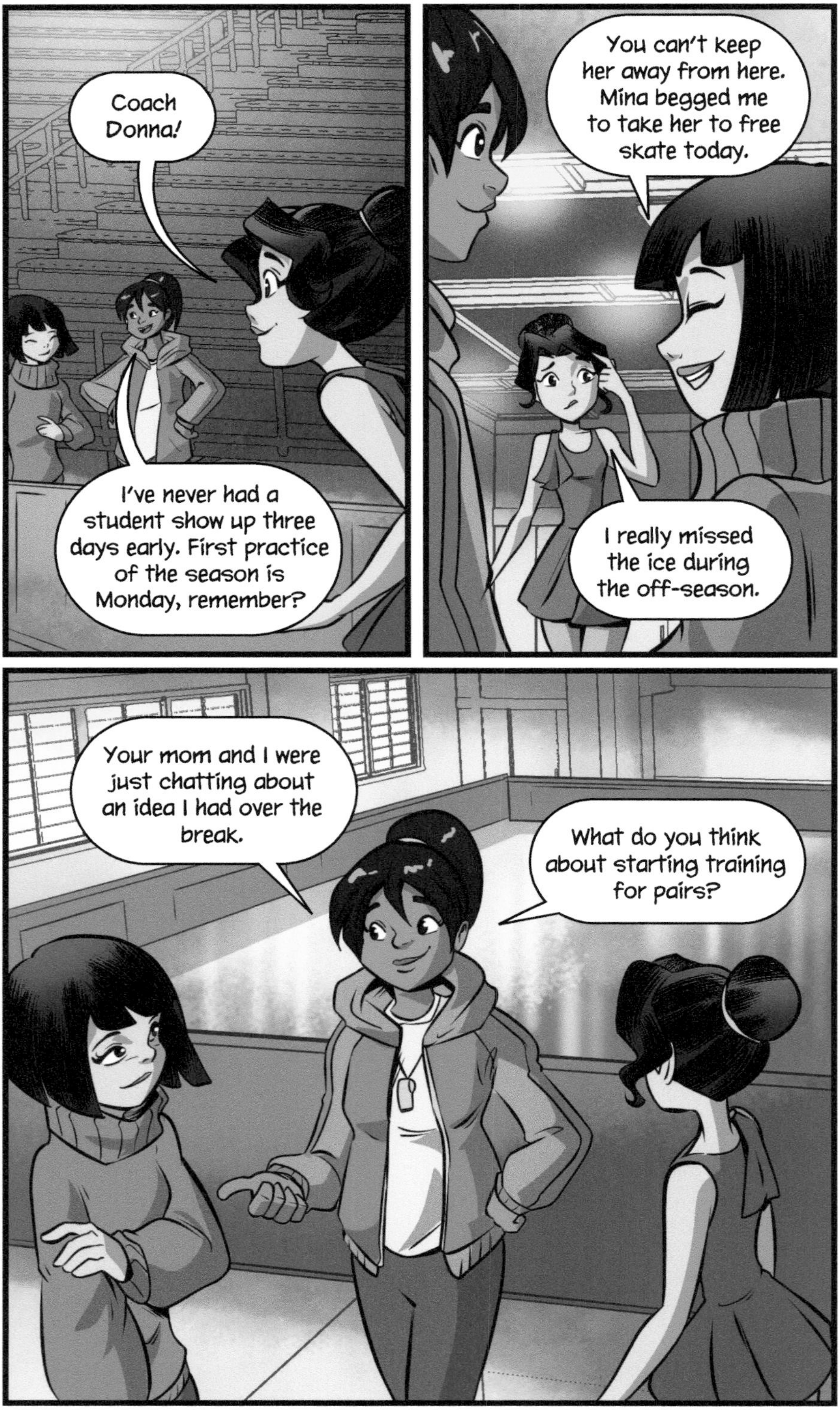
Coach Donna!
I've never had a student show up three days early. First practice of the season is Monday, remember?
You can't keep her away from here. Mina begged me to take her to free skate today.
I really missed the ice during the off-season.
Your mom and I were just chatting about an idea I had over the break.
What do you think about starting training for pairs?

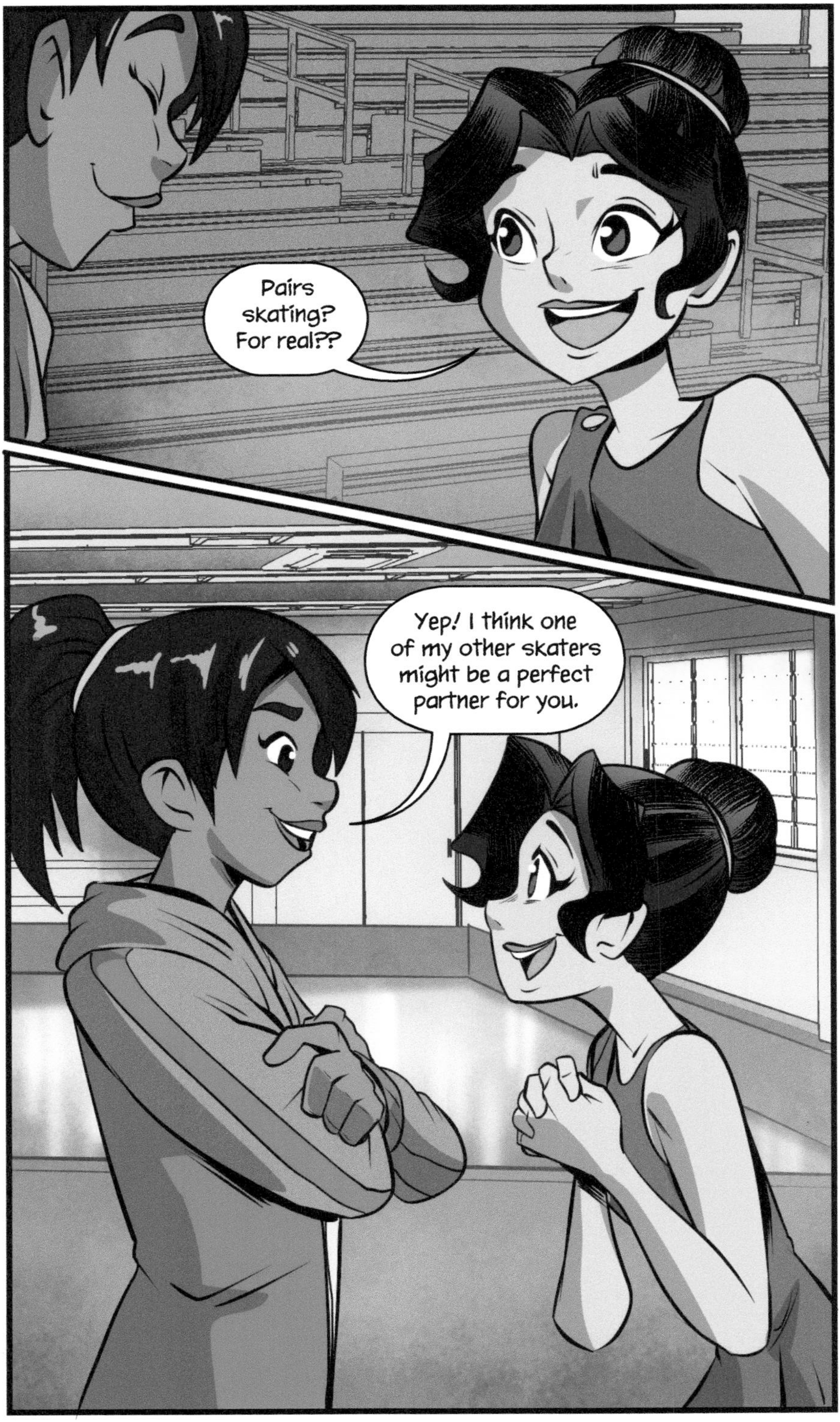
Pairs skating? For real??
Yep! I think one of my other skaters might be a perfect partner for you.

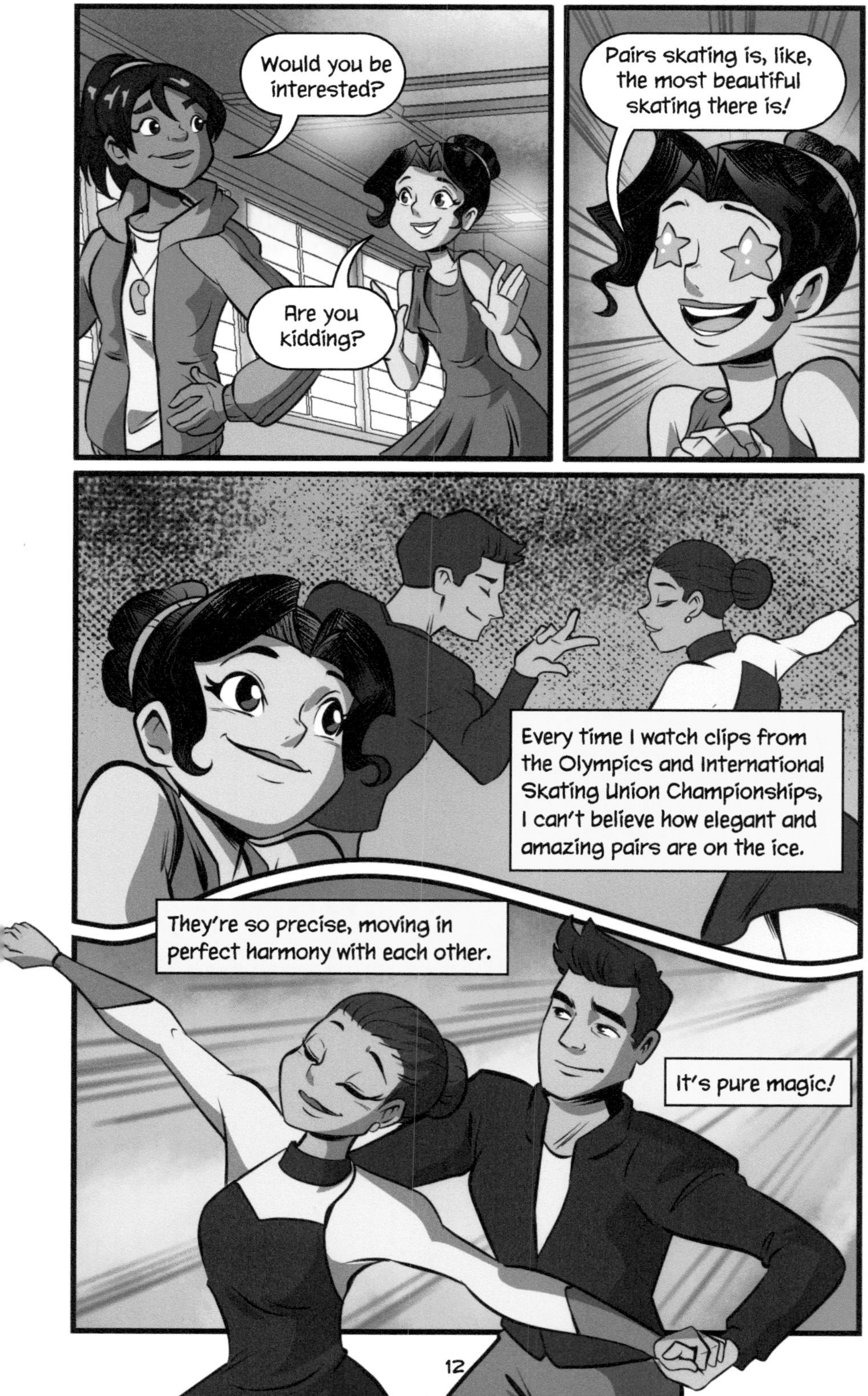
Would you be interested?
Are you kidding?
Pairs skating is, like, the most beautiful skating there is!
Every time I watch clips from the Olympics and International Skating Union Championships, I can't believe how elegant and amazing pairs are on the ice.
They're so precise, moving in perfect harmony with each other.
It's pure magic!

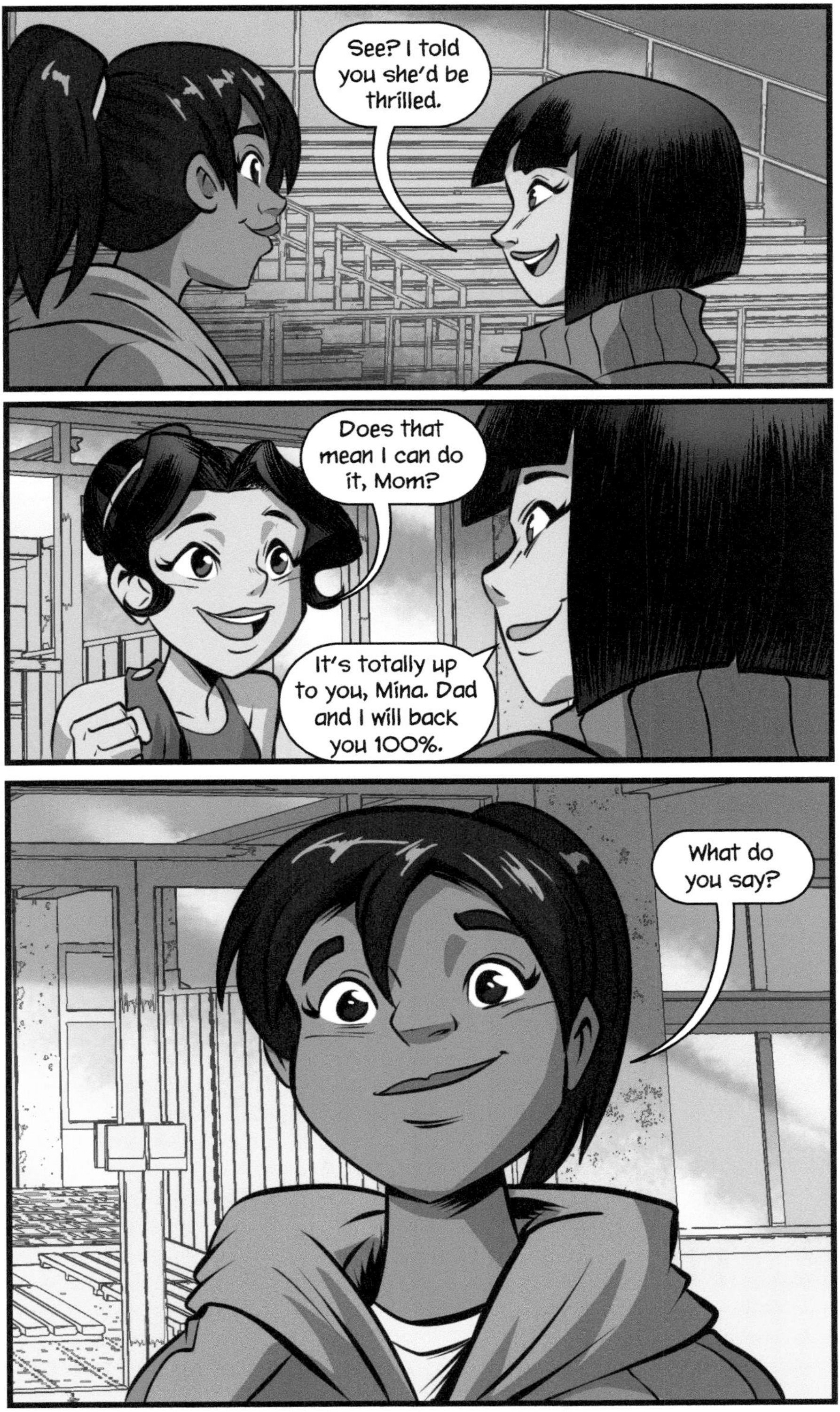
See? I told you she'd be thrilled.
Does that mean I can do it, Mom?
It's totally up to you, Mina. Dad and I will back you 100%.
What do you say?

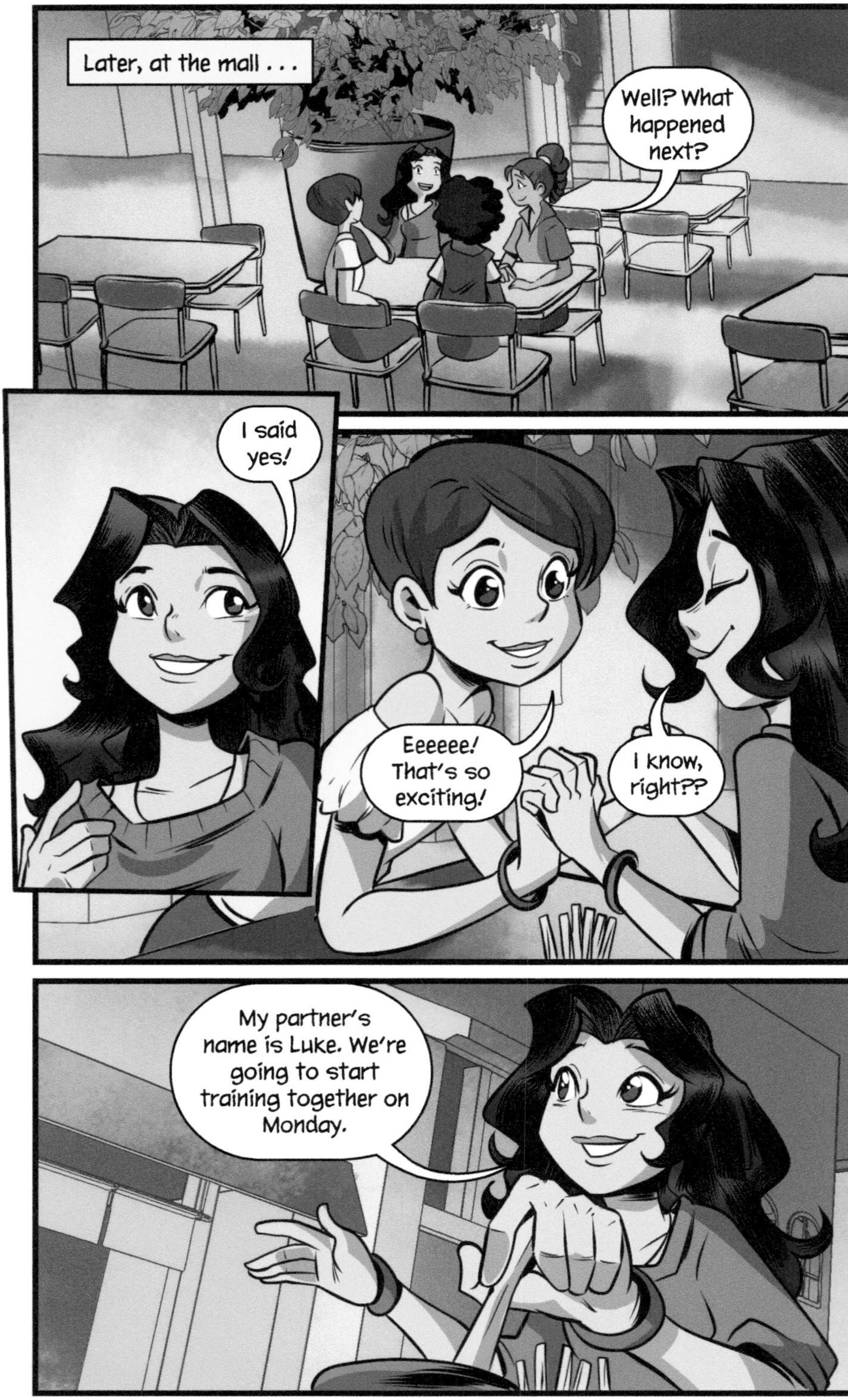

Later, at the mall . . .
Well? What happened next?
I said yes!
Eeeeee! That's so exciting!
I know, right??
My partner's name is Luke. We're going to start training together on Monday.

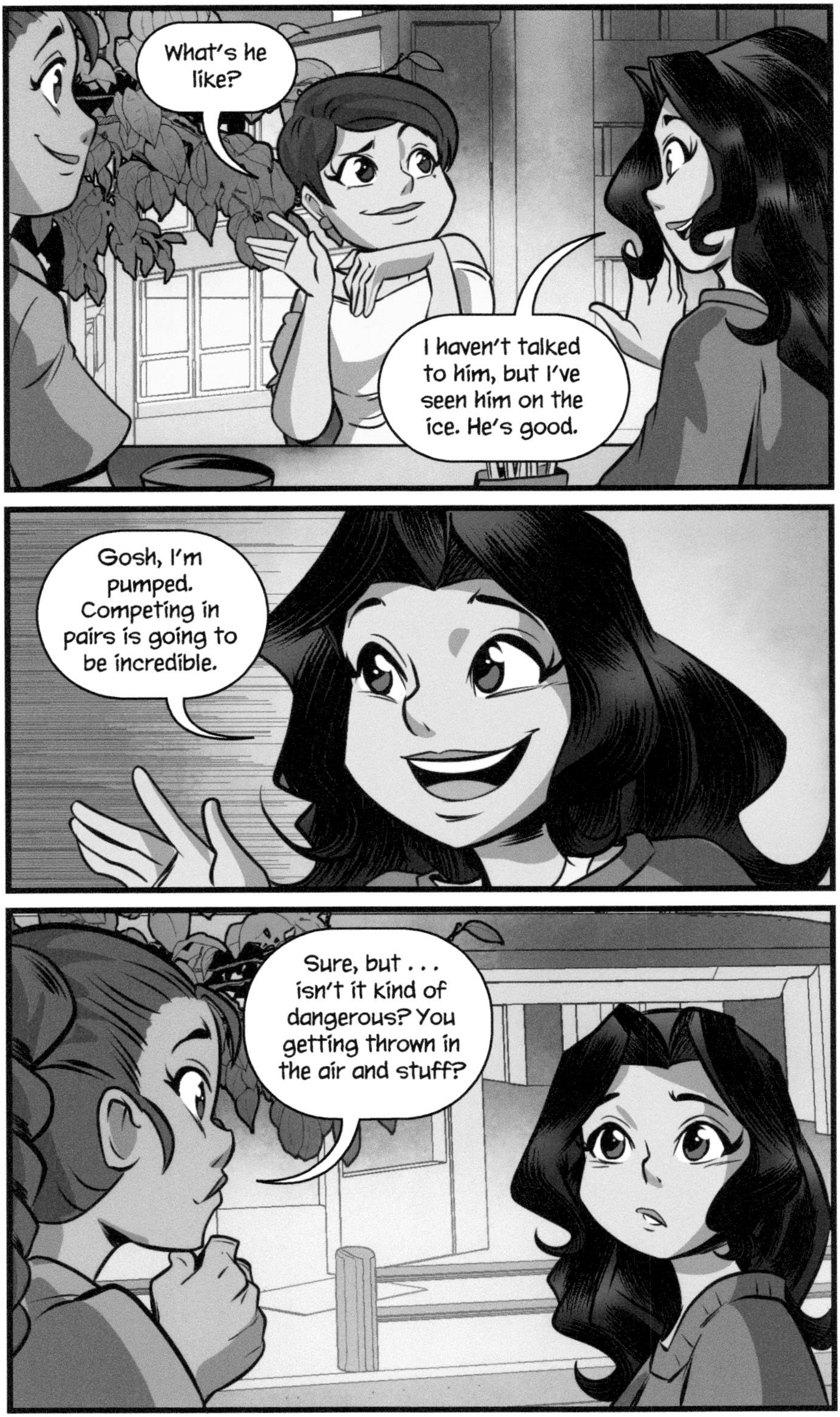
What's he like?
I haven't talked to him, but I've seen him on the ice. He's good.
Gosh, I'm pumped. Competing in pairs is going to be incredible.
Sure, but . . . isn't it kind of dangerous? You getting thrown in the air and stuff?

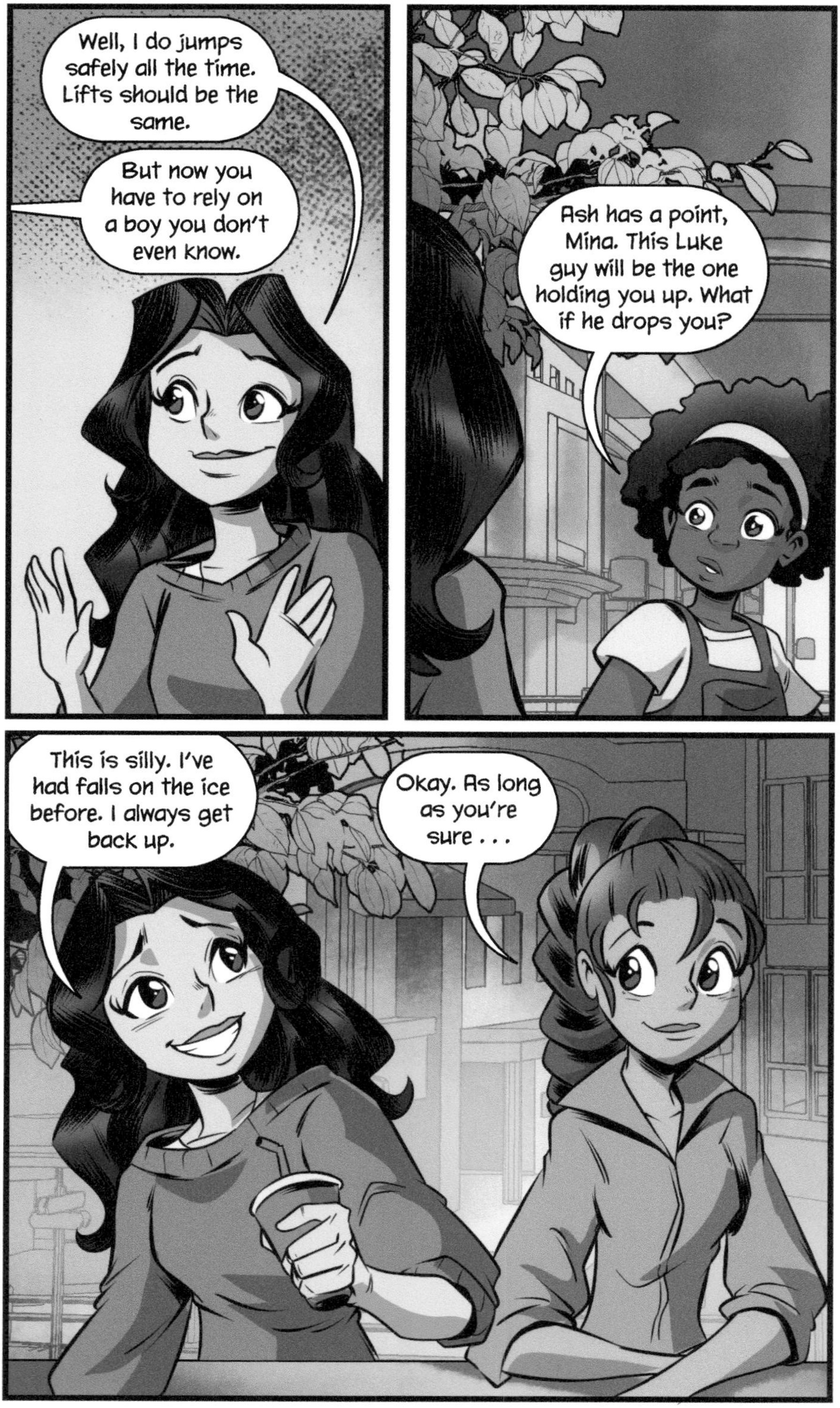
Well, I do jumps safely all the time. Lifts should be the same.
But now you have to rely on a boy you don't even know.
Ash has a point, Mina. This Luke guy will be the one holding you up. What if he drops you?
This is silly. I've had falls on the ice before. I always get back up.
Okay. As long as you're sure . . .

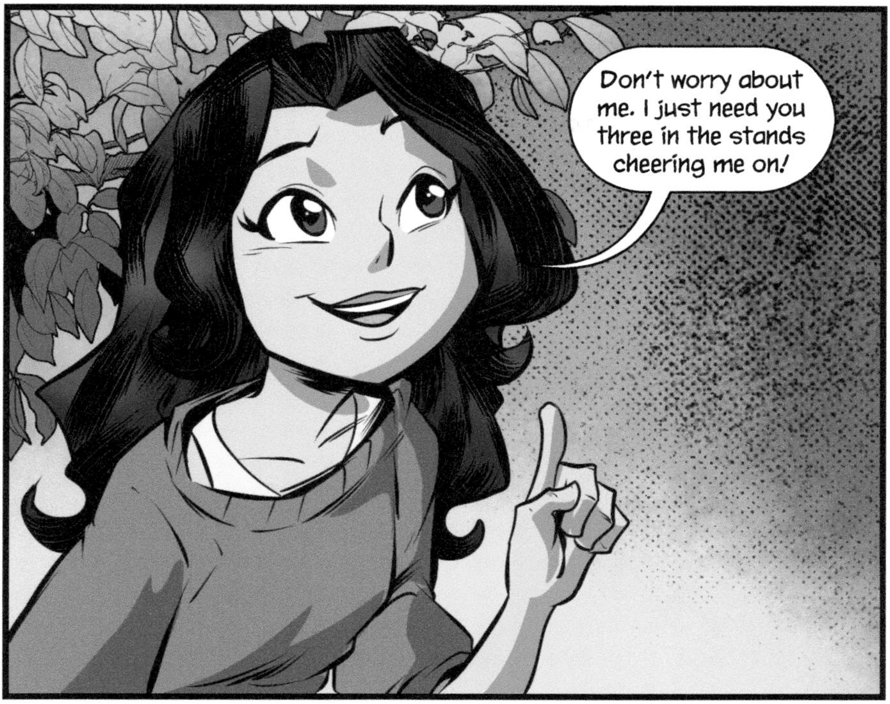
Don't worry about me. I just need you three in the stands cheering me on!

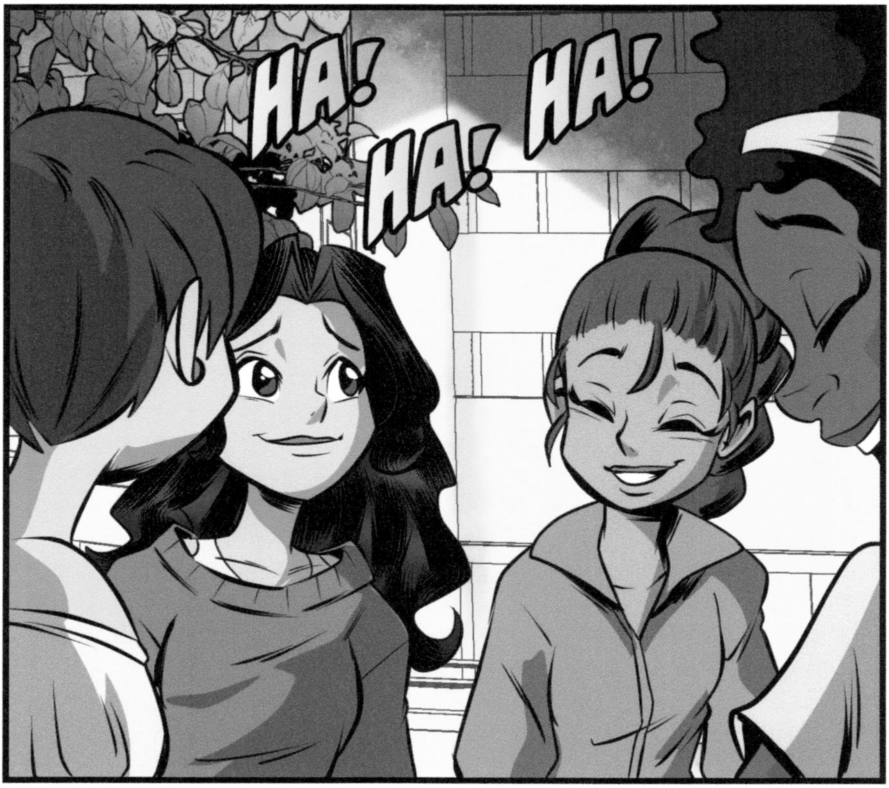
HA!
HA!
HA!

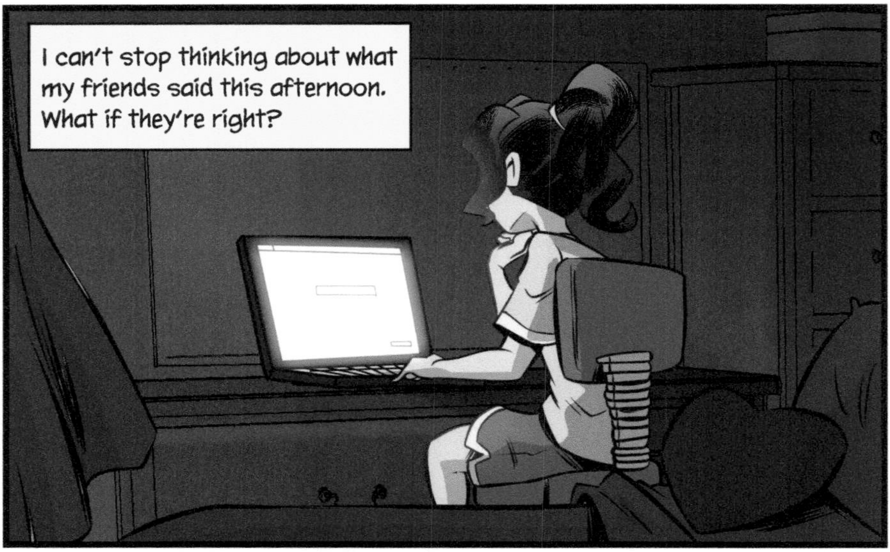
I can't stop thinking about what my friends said this afternoon. What if they're right?

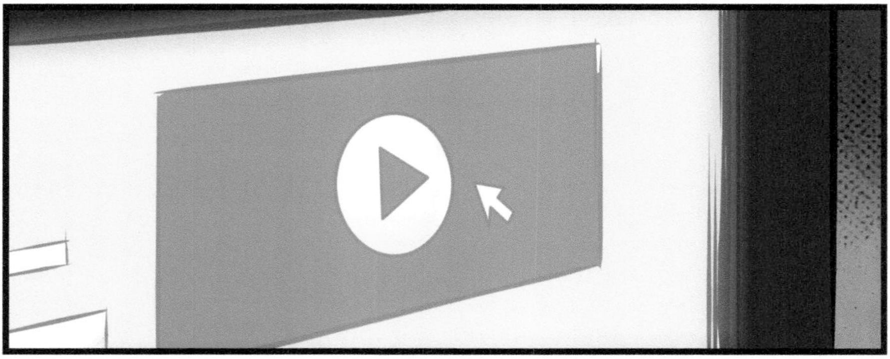

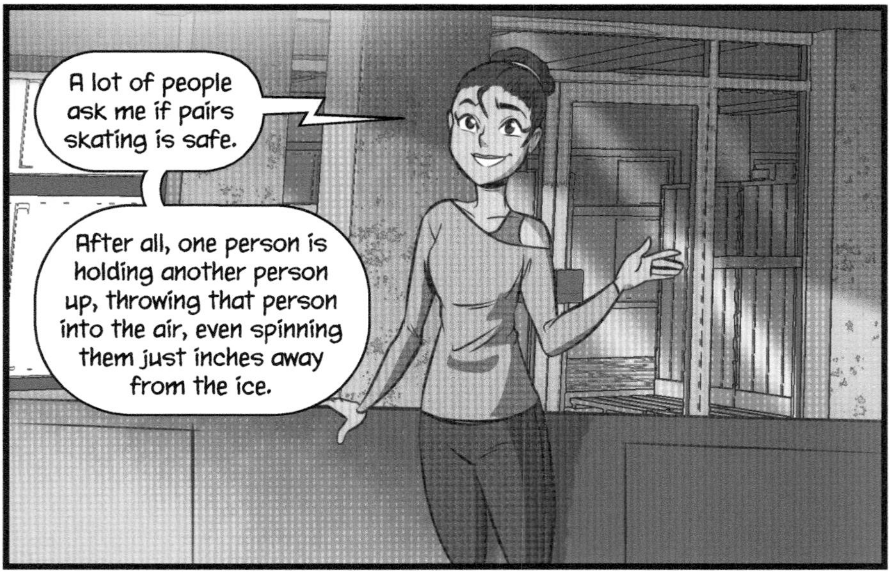
A lot of people ask me if pairs skating is safe.
After all, one person is holding another person up, throwing that person into the air, even spinning them just inches away from the ice.

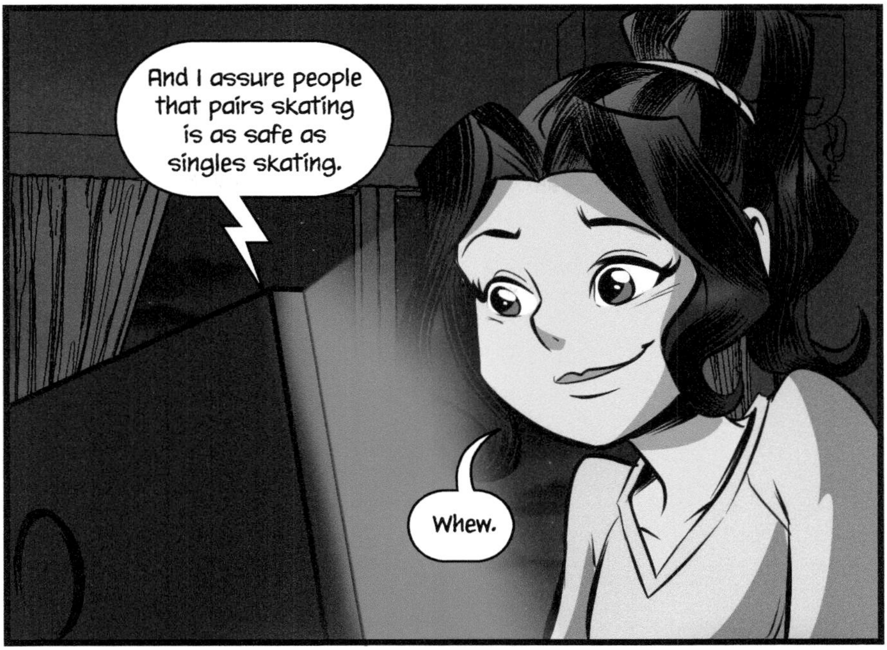
And I assure people that pairs skating is as safe as singles skating.
Whew.

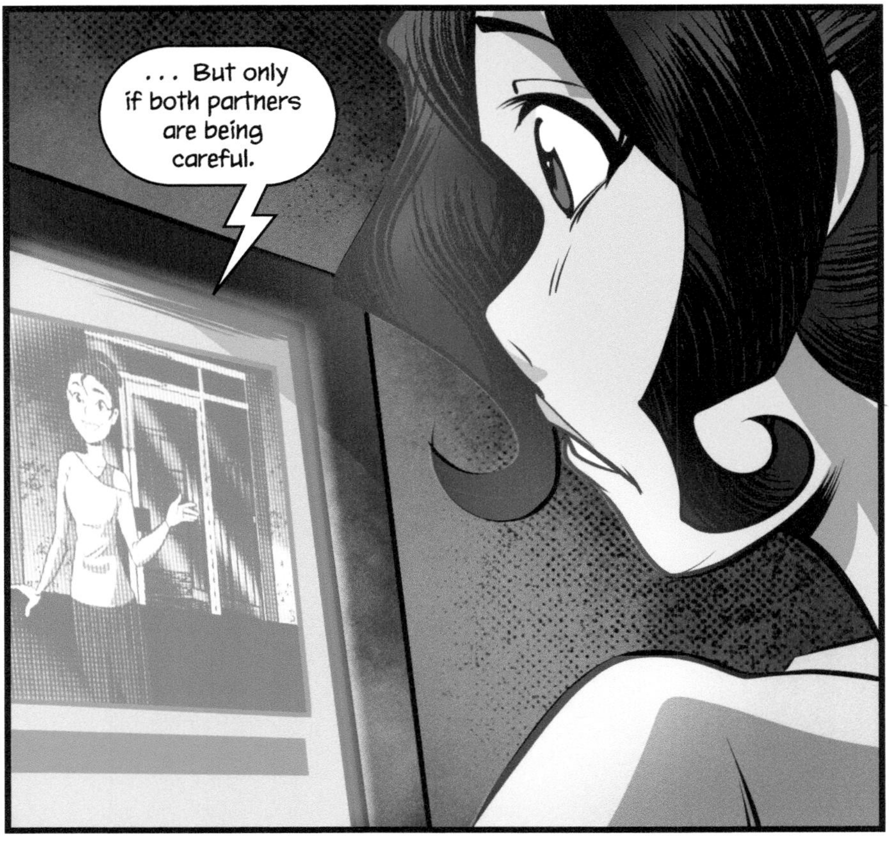
. . . But only if both partners are being careful.

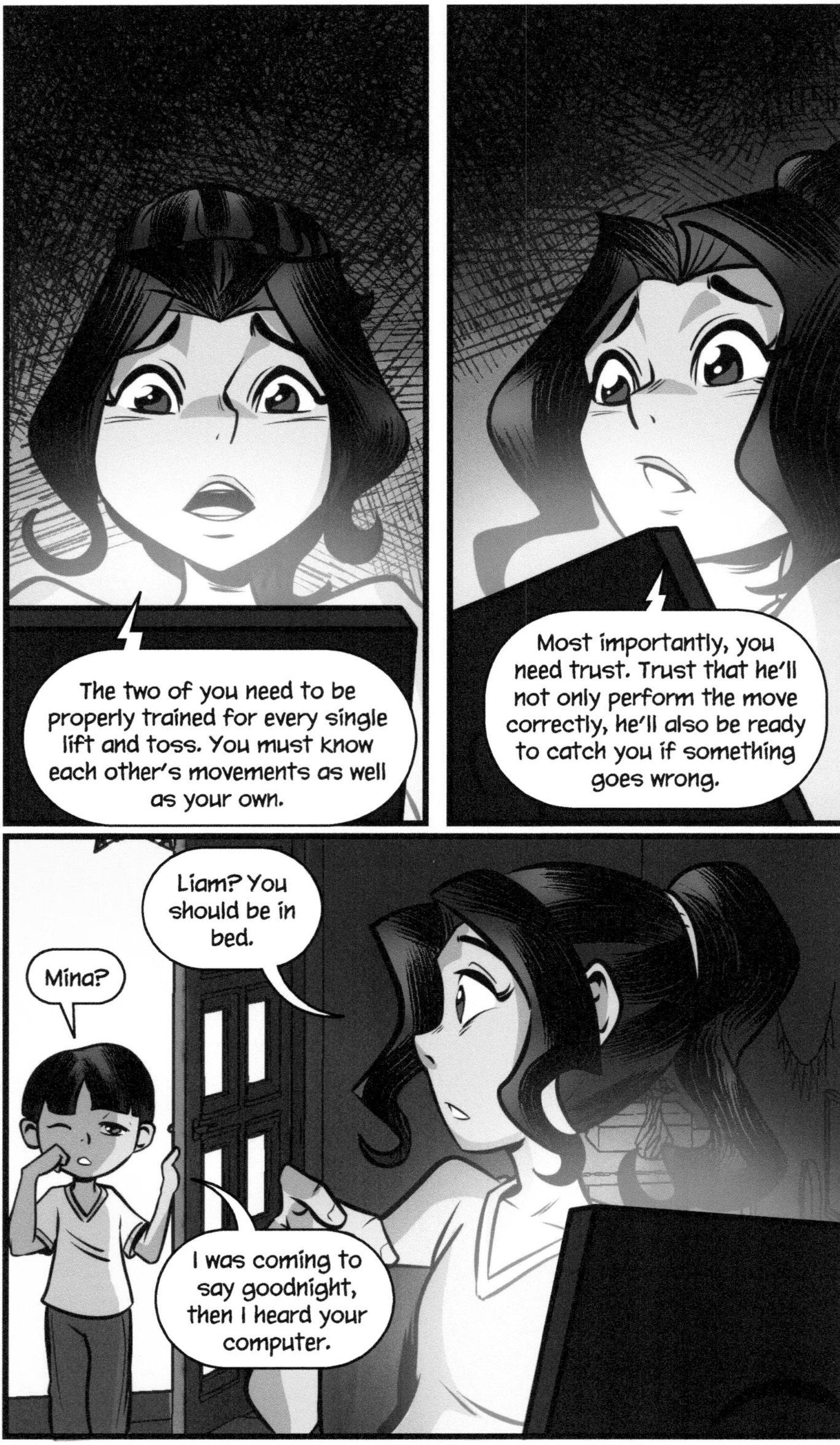
The two of you need to be properly trained for every single lift and toss. You must know each other's movements as well as your own.
Most importantly, you need trust. Trust that he'll not only perform the move correctly, he'll also be ready to catch you if something goes wrong.
Mina?
Liam? You should be in bed.
I was coming to say goodnight, then I heard your computer.

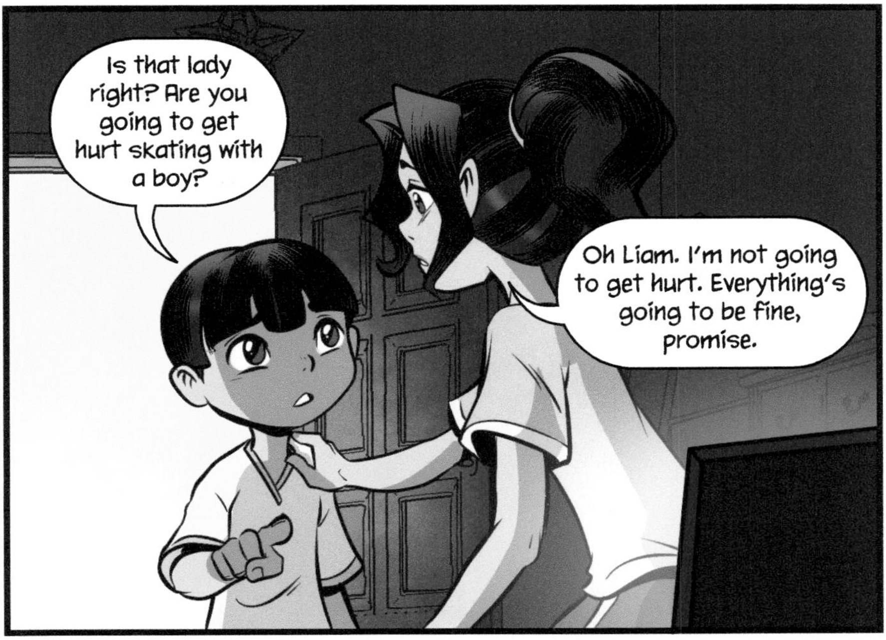
Is that lady right? Are you going to get hurt skating with a boy?
Oh Liam. I'm not going to get hurt. Everything's going to be fine, promise.

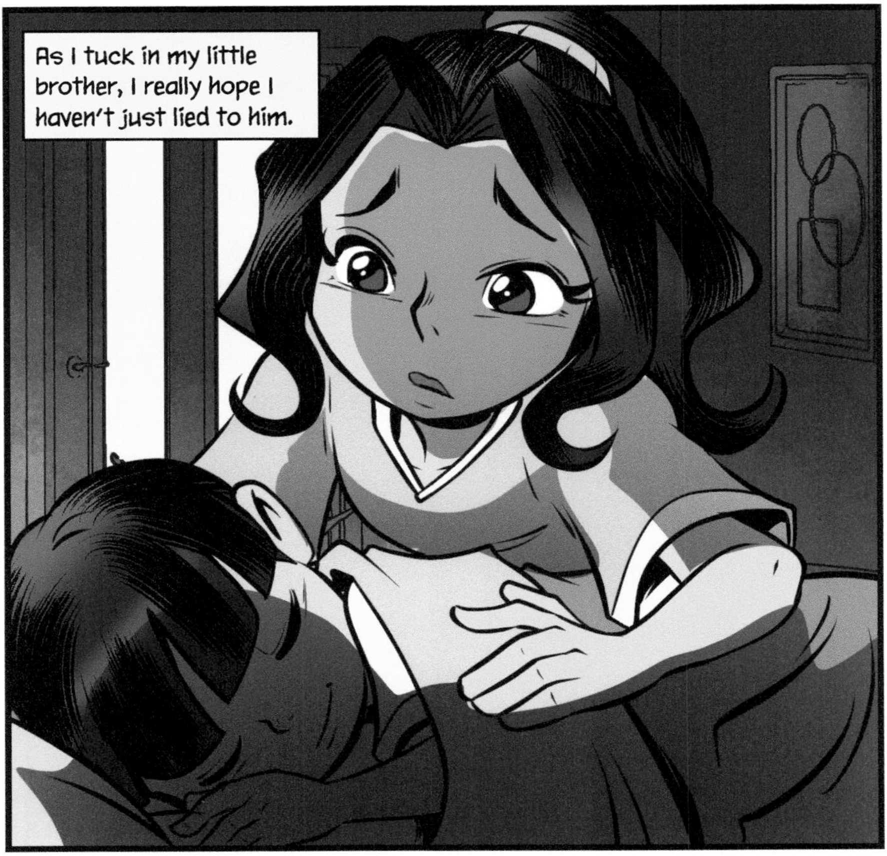
As I tuck in my little brother, I really hope I haven't just lied to him.

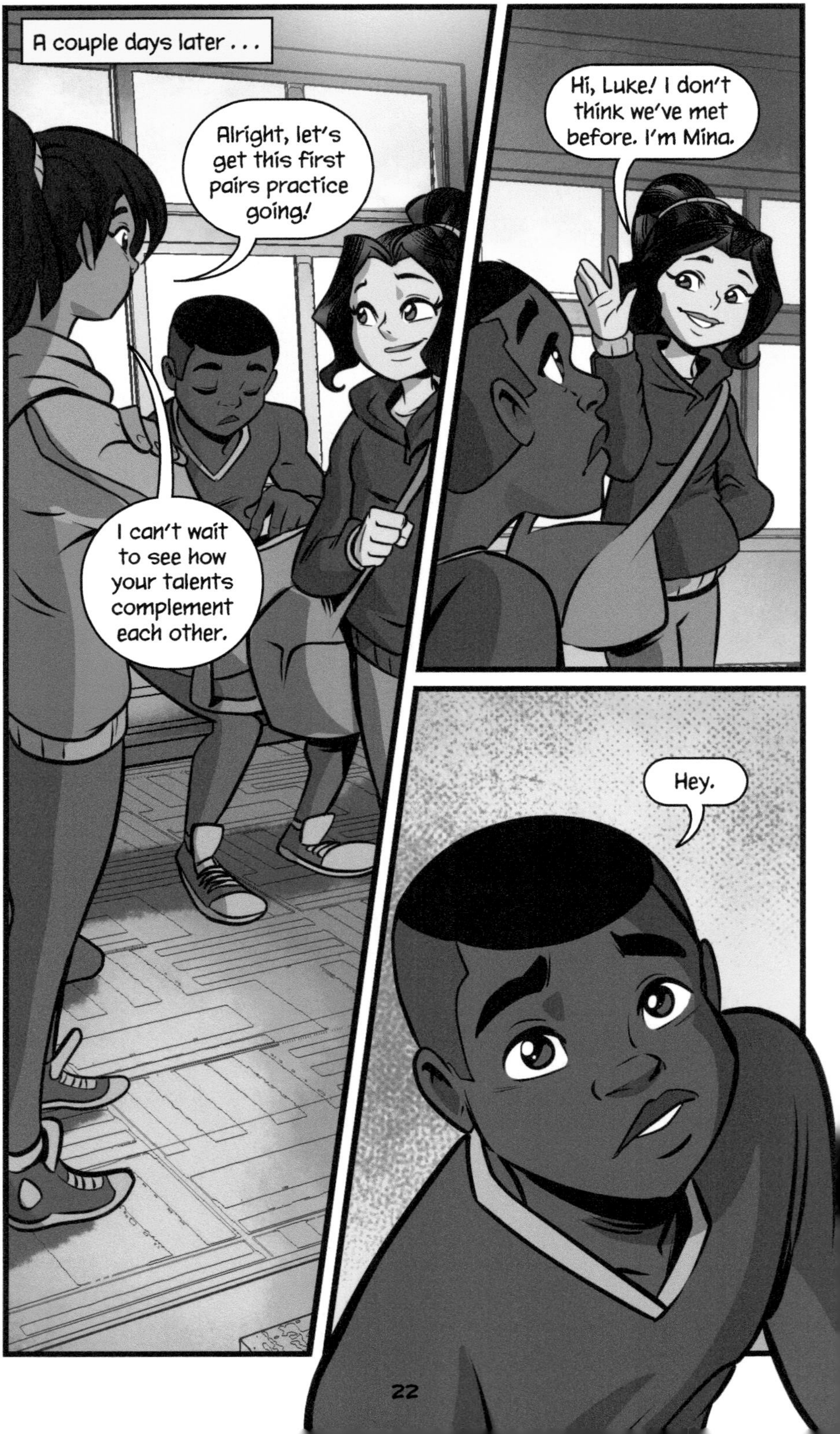
A couple days later . . .
Alright, let's get this first pairs practice going!
I can't wait to see how your talents complement each other.
Hi, Luke! I don't think we've met before. I'm Mina.
Hey.

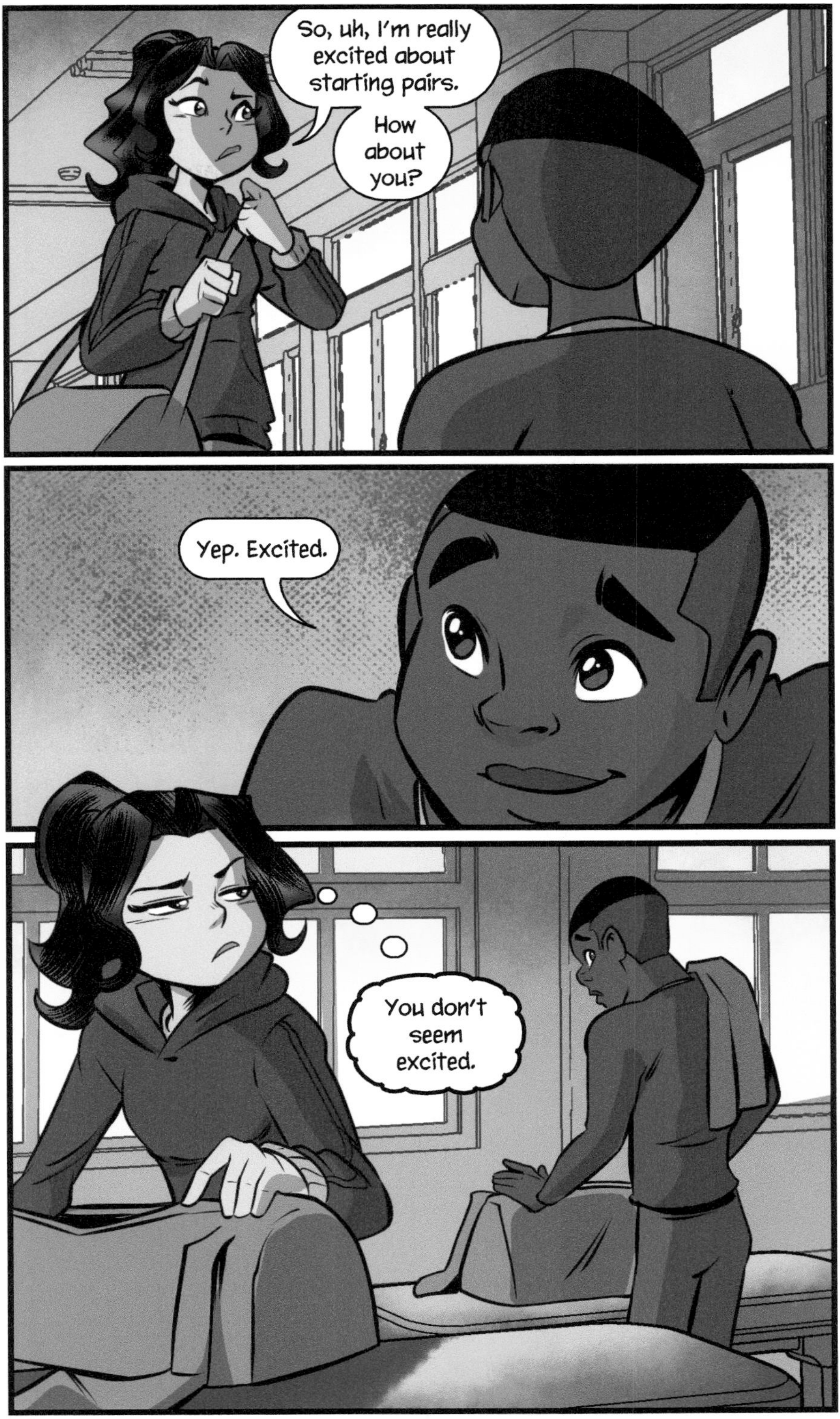
So, uh, I'm really excited about starting pairs.
How about you?
Yep. Excited.
You don't seem excited.

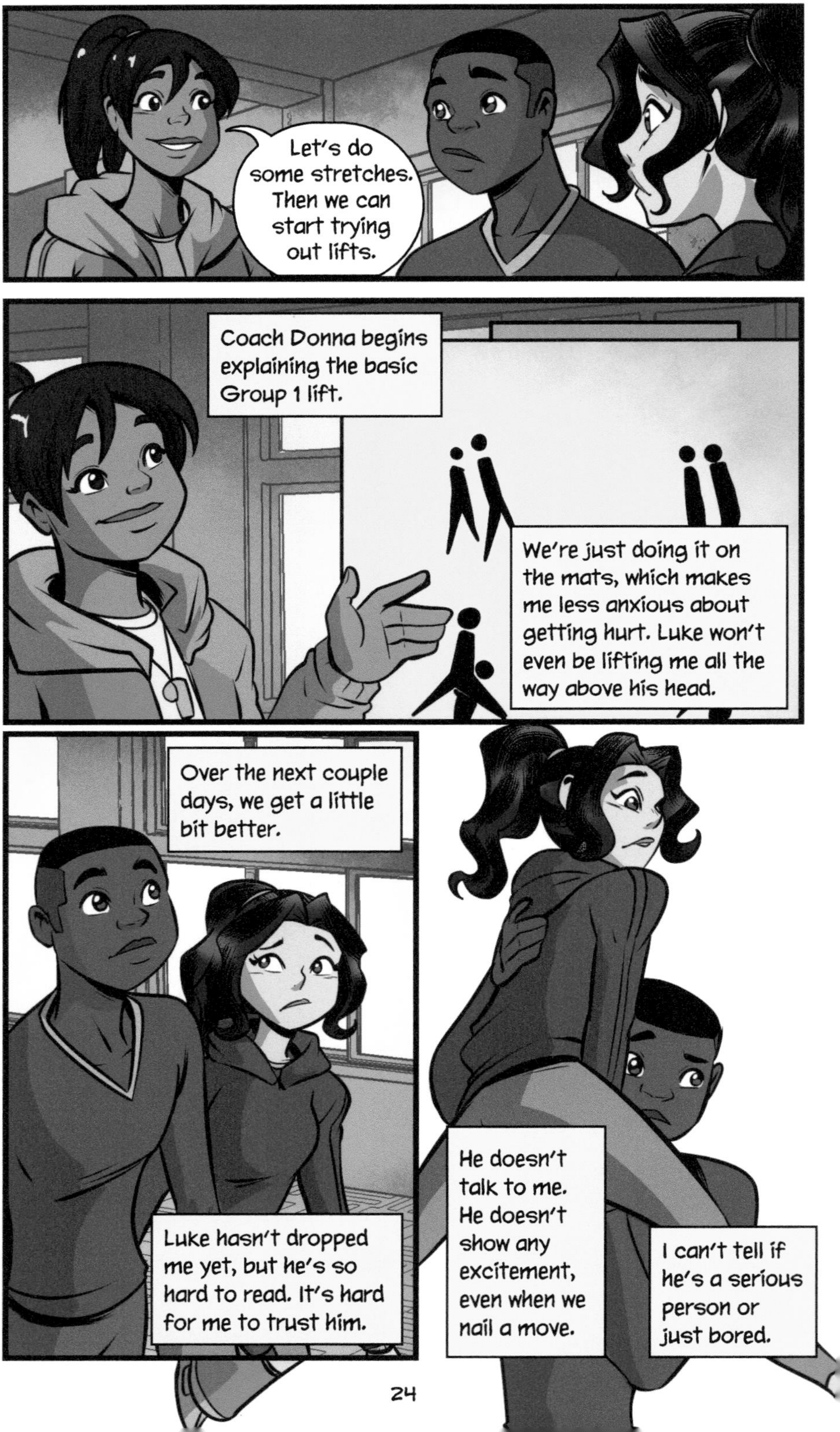
Let's do some stretches. Then we can start trying out lifts.
Coach Donna begins explaining the basic Group 1 lift.
We're just doing it on the mats, which makes me less anxious about getting hurt. Luke won't even be lifting me all the way above his head.
Over the next couple days, we get a little bit better.
Luke hasn't dropped me yet, but he's so hard to read. It's hard for me to trust him.
He doesn't talk to me. He doesn't show any excitement, even when we nail a move.
I can't tell if he's a serious person or just bored.

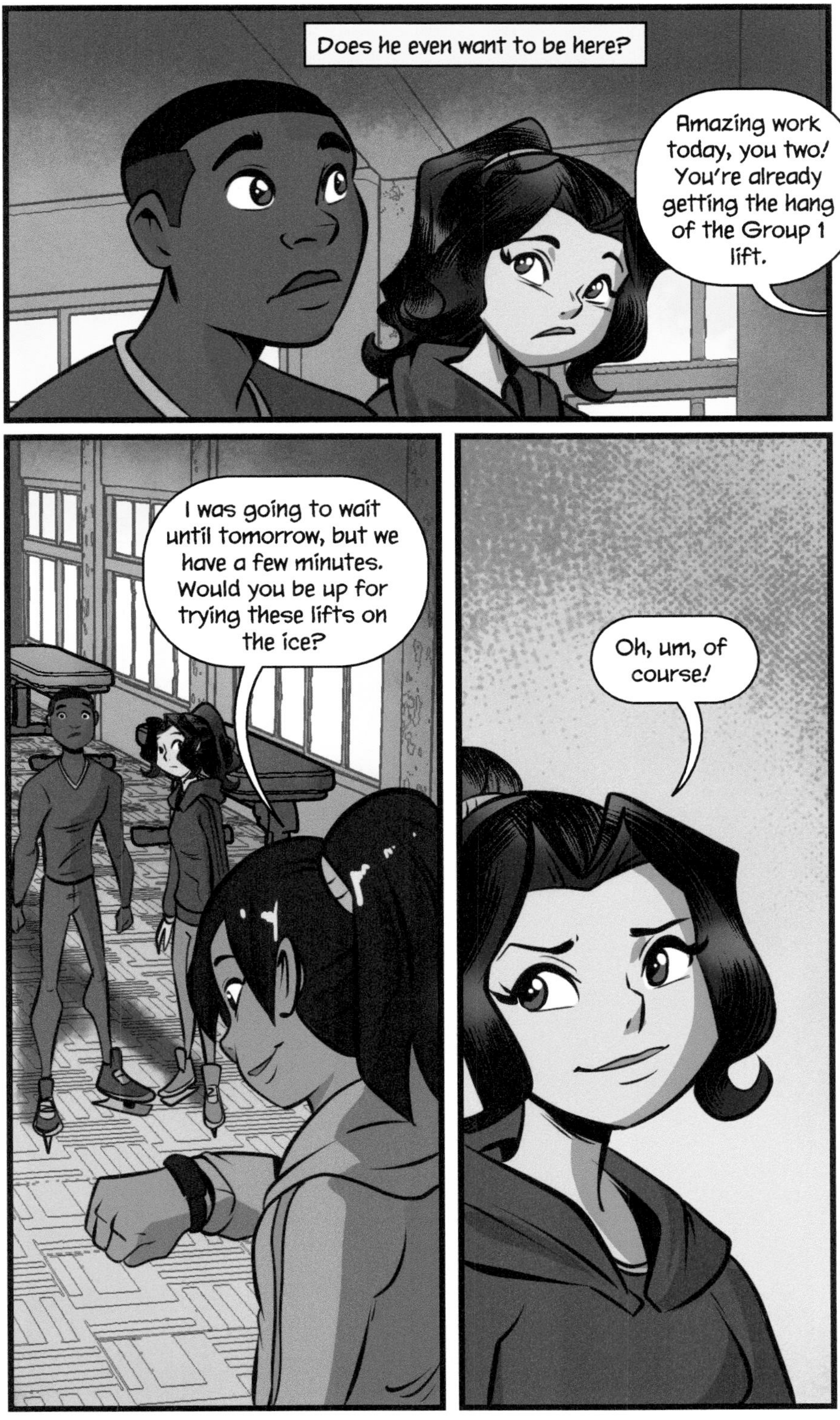
Does he even want to be here?
Amazing work today, you two! You're already getting the hang of the Group 1 lift.
I was going to wait until tomorrow, but we have a few minutes. Would you be up for trying these lifts on the ice?
Oh, um, of course!

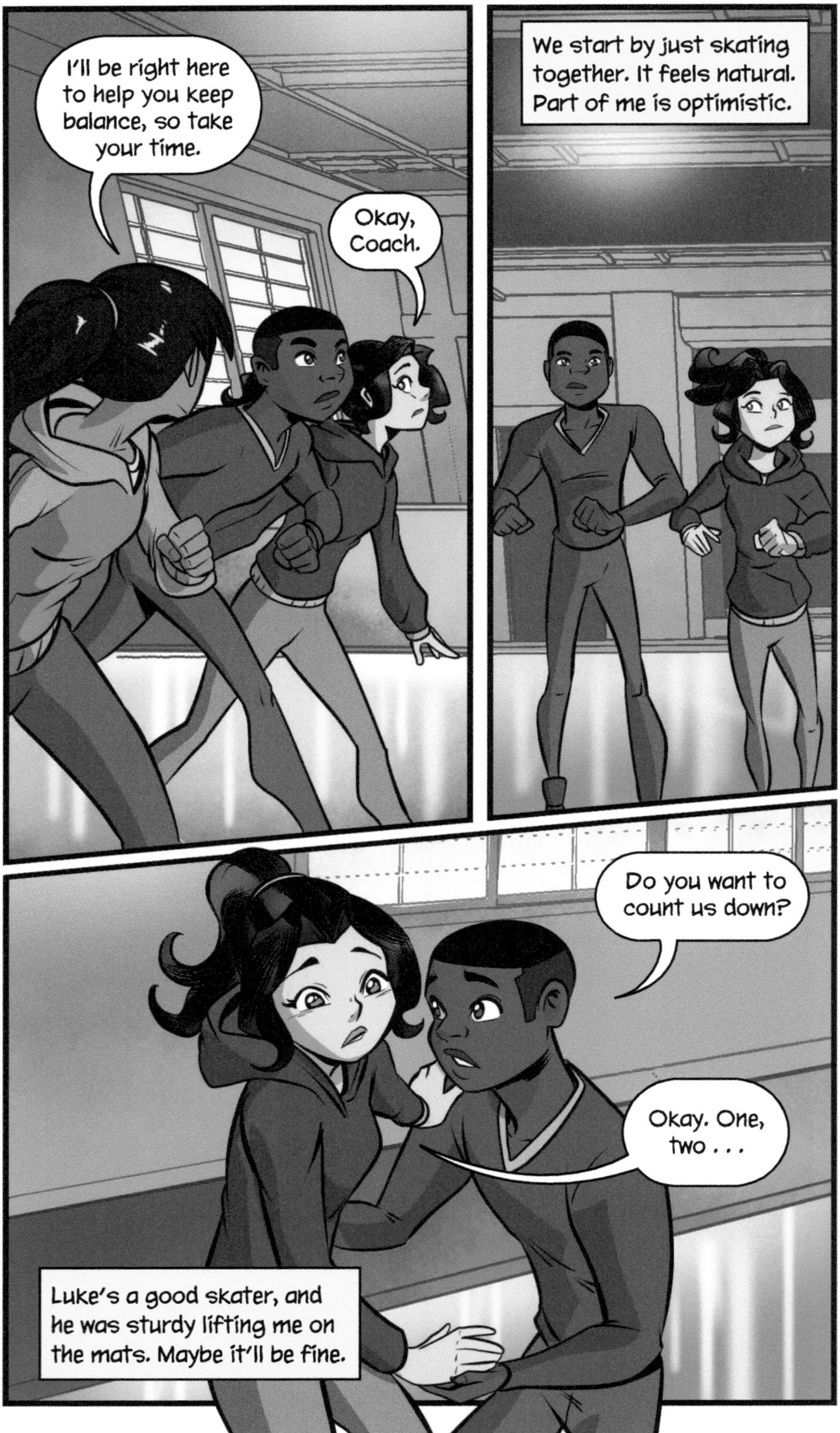
I'll be right here to help you keep balance, so take your time.
Okay, Coach.
We start by just skating together. It feels natural. Part of me is optimistic.
Do you want to count us down?
Okay. One, two . . .
Luke's a good skater, and he was sturdy lifting me on the mats. Maybe it'll be fine.

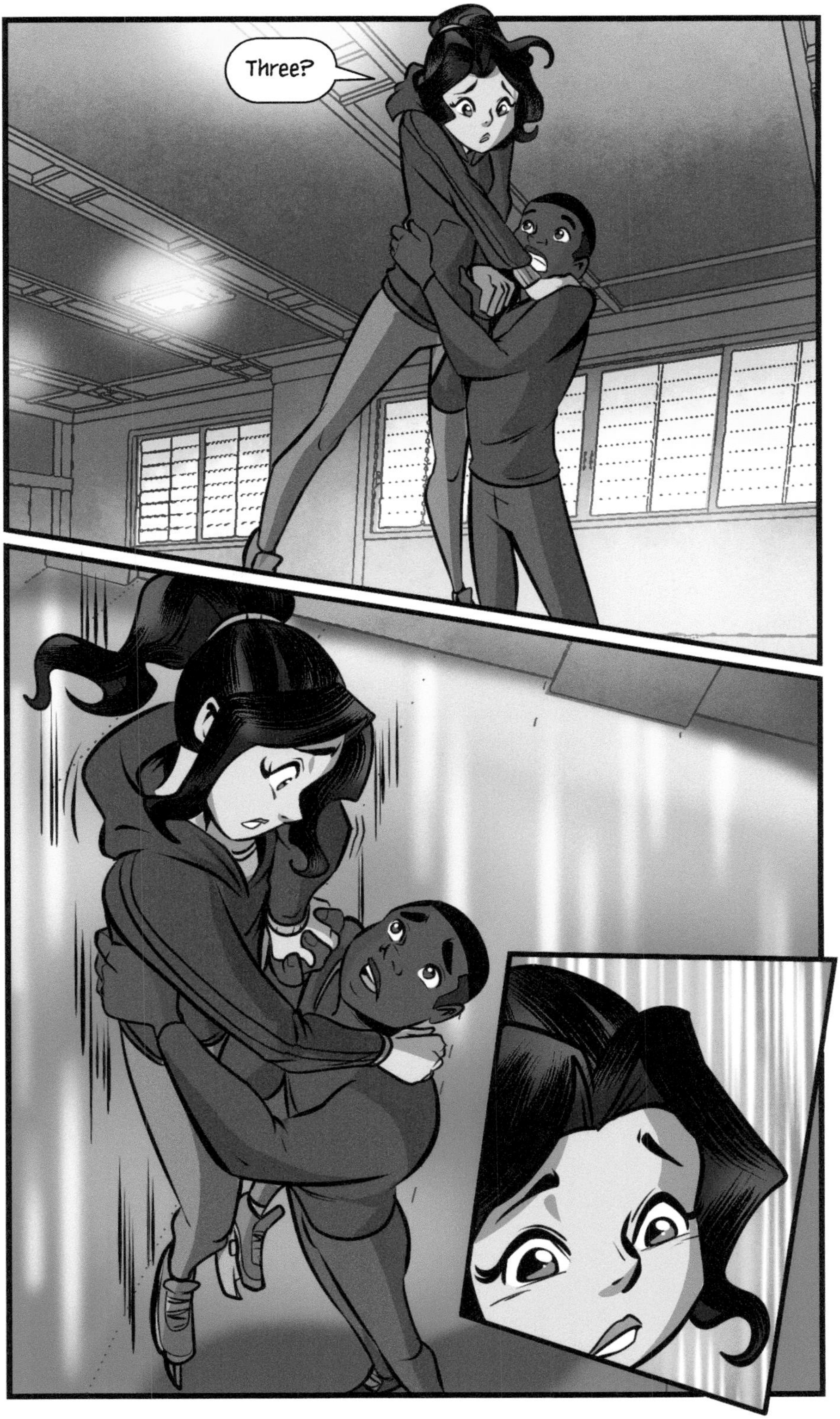
Three?

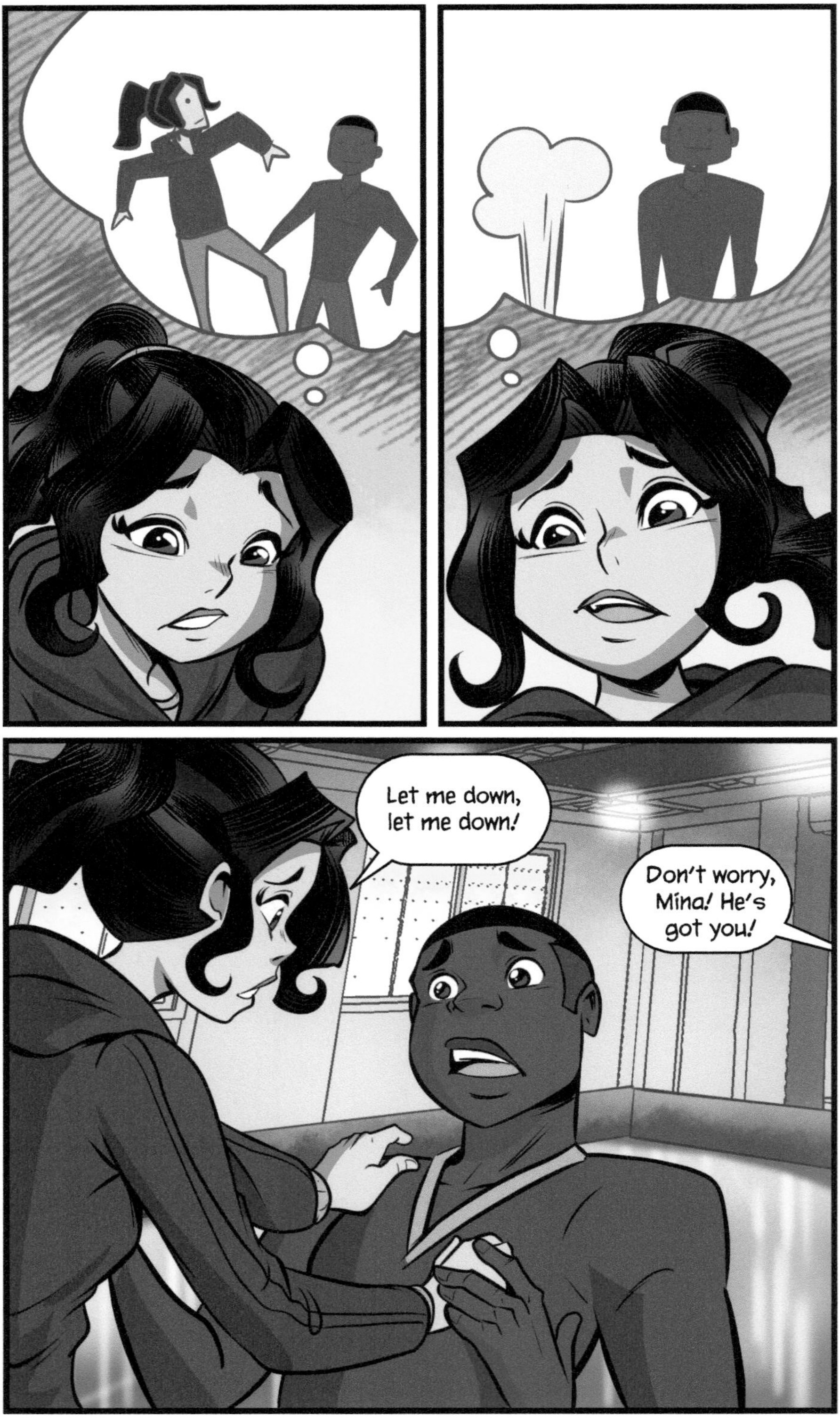

Let me down, let me down!
Don't worry, Mina! He's got you!

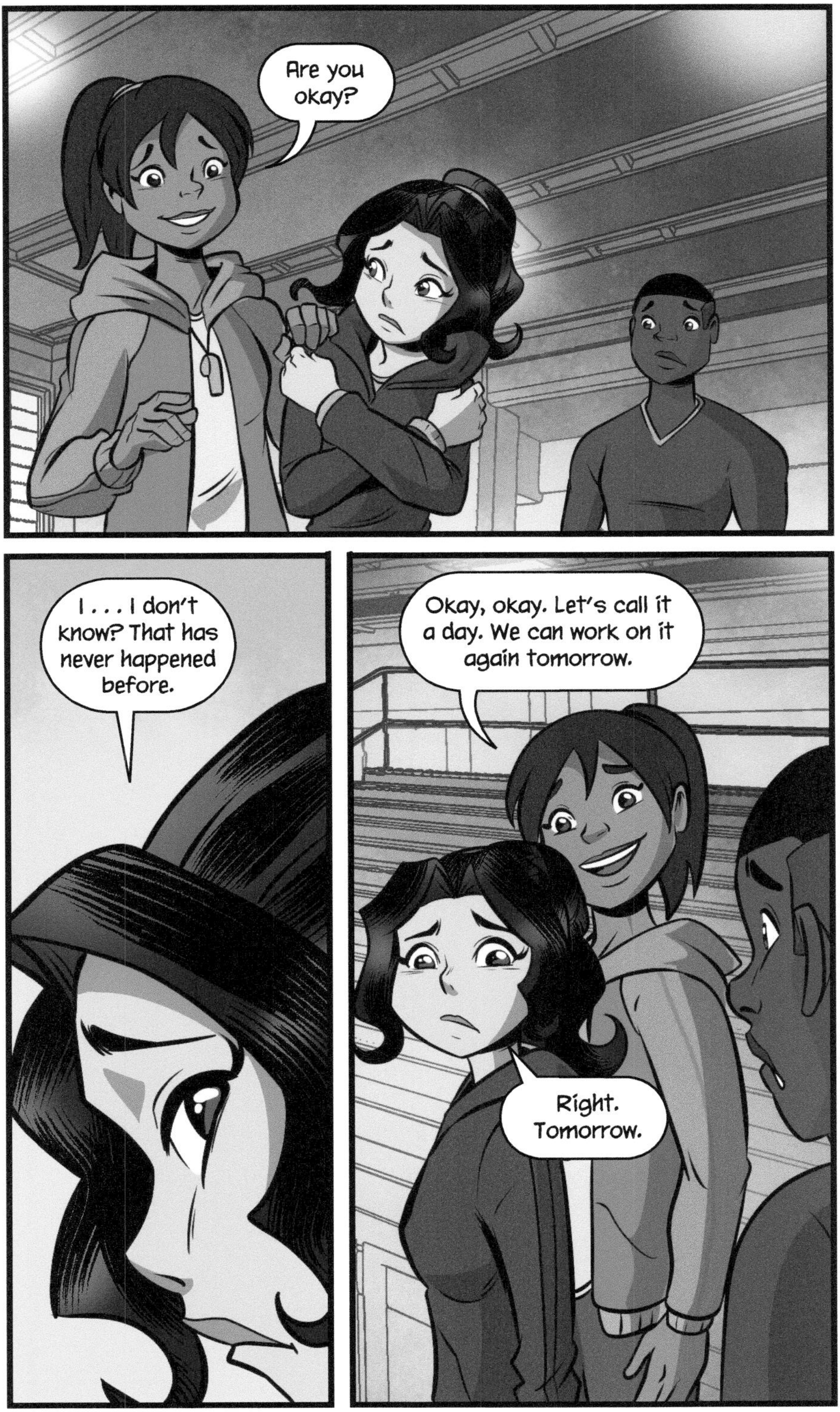
Are you okay?
I . . . I don't know? That has never happened before.
Okay, okay. Let's call it a day. We can work on it again tomorrow.
Right. Tomorrow.

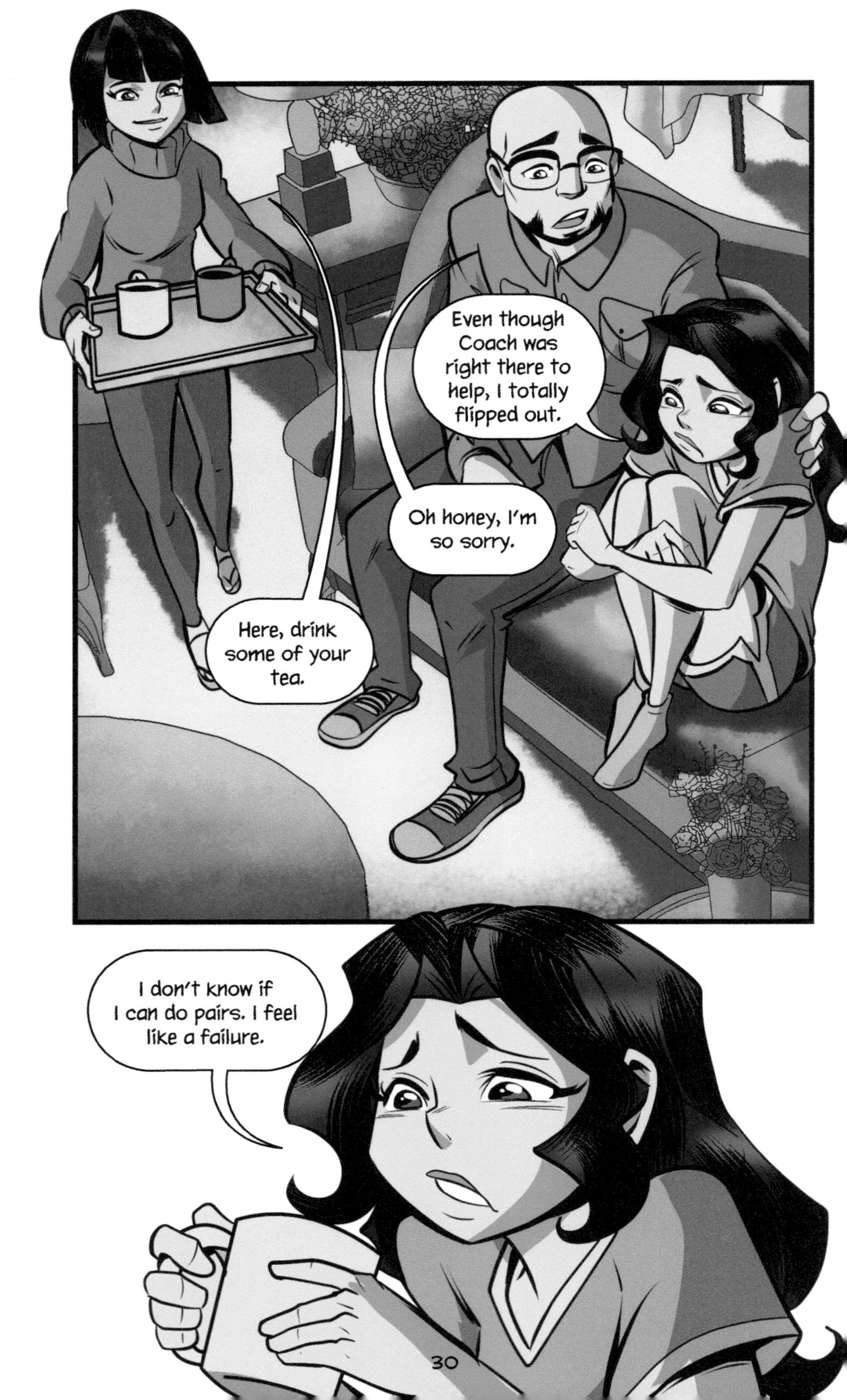
Even though Coach was right there to help, I totally flipped out.
Oh honey, I'm so sorry.
Here, drink some of your tea.
I don't know if I can do pairs. I feel like a failure.

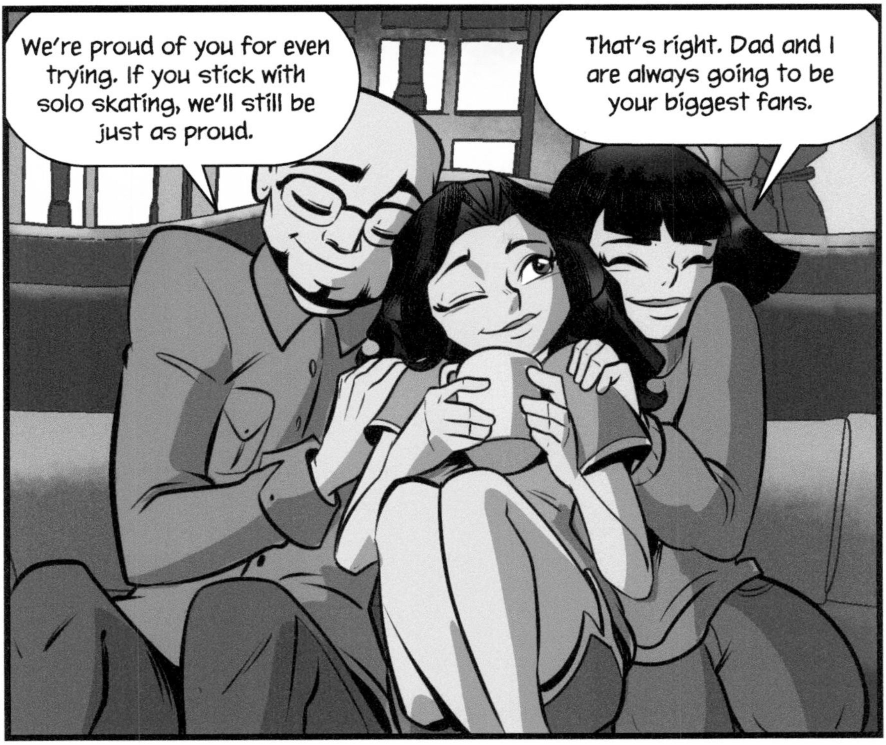
We're proud of you for even trying. If you stick with solo skating, we'll still be just as proud.
That's right. Dad and I are always going to be your biggest fans.

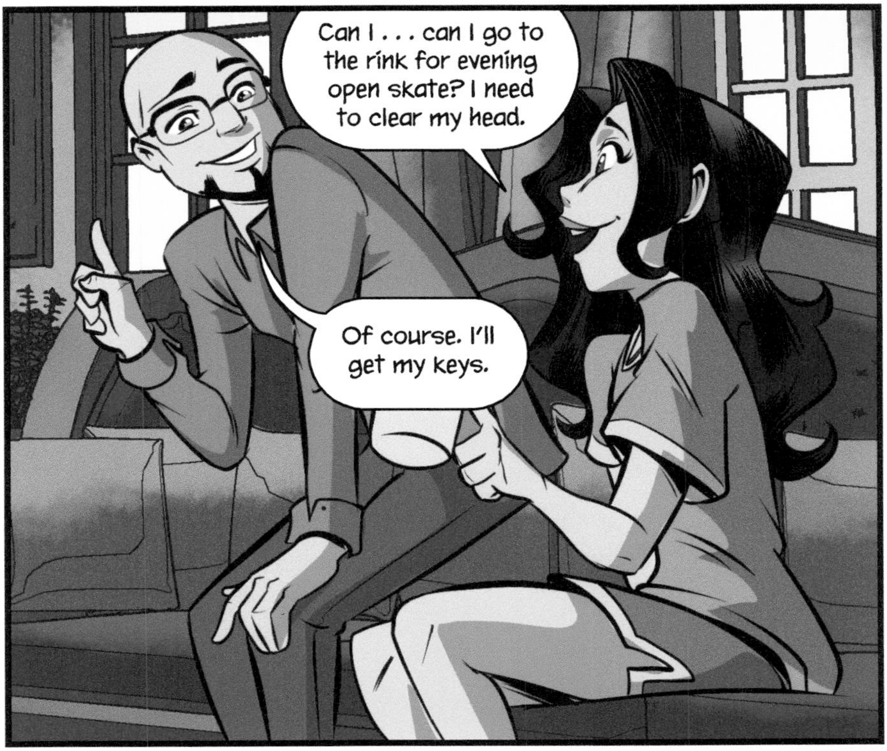
Can I . . . can I go to the rink for evening open skate? I need to clear my head.
Of course. I'll get my keys.

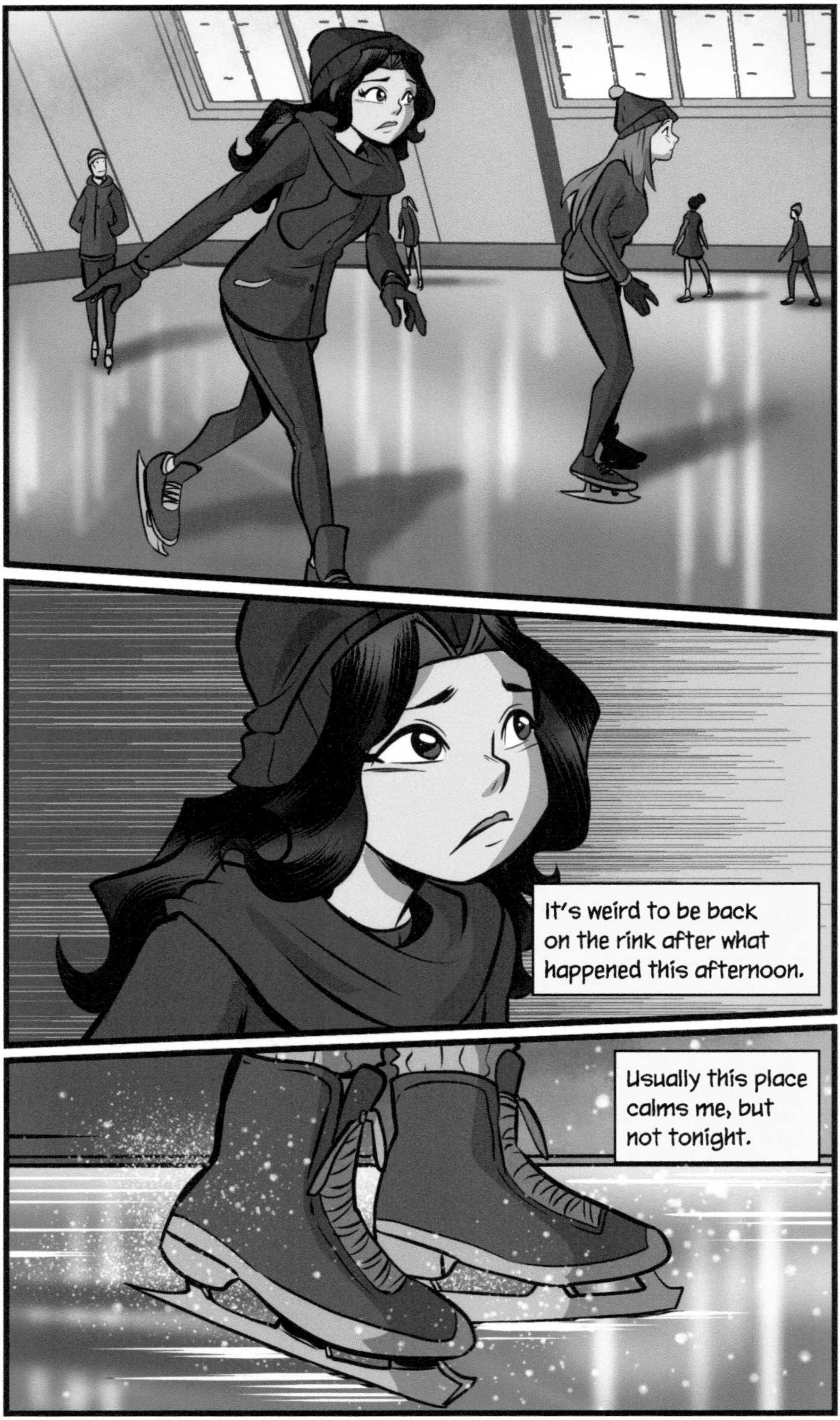
It's weird to be back on the rink after what happened this afternoon.
Usually this place calms me, but not tonight.

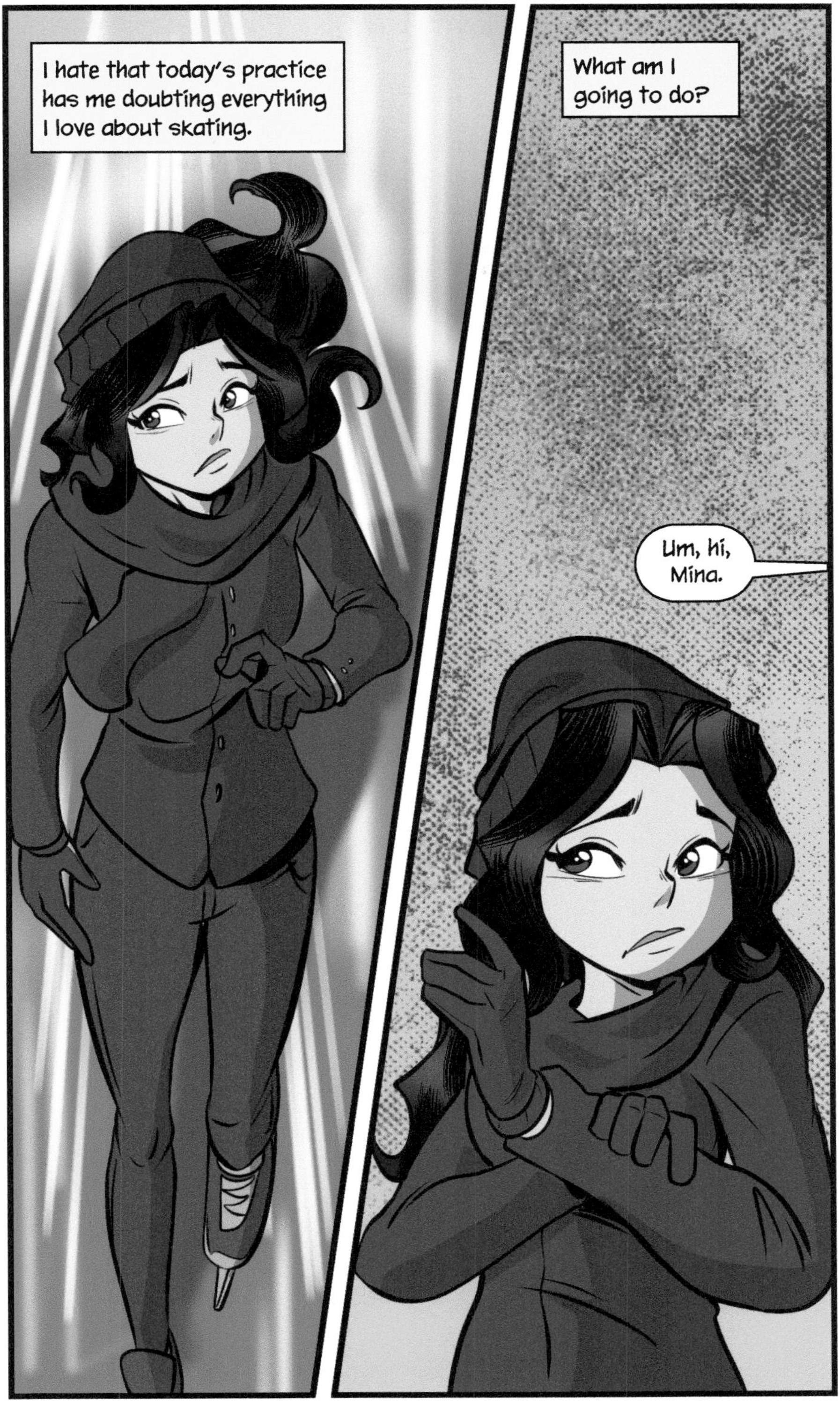
I hate that today's practice has me doubting everything I love about skating.
What am I going to do?
Um, hi, Mina.

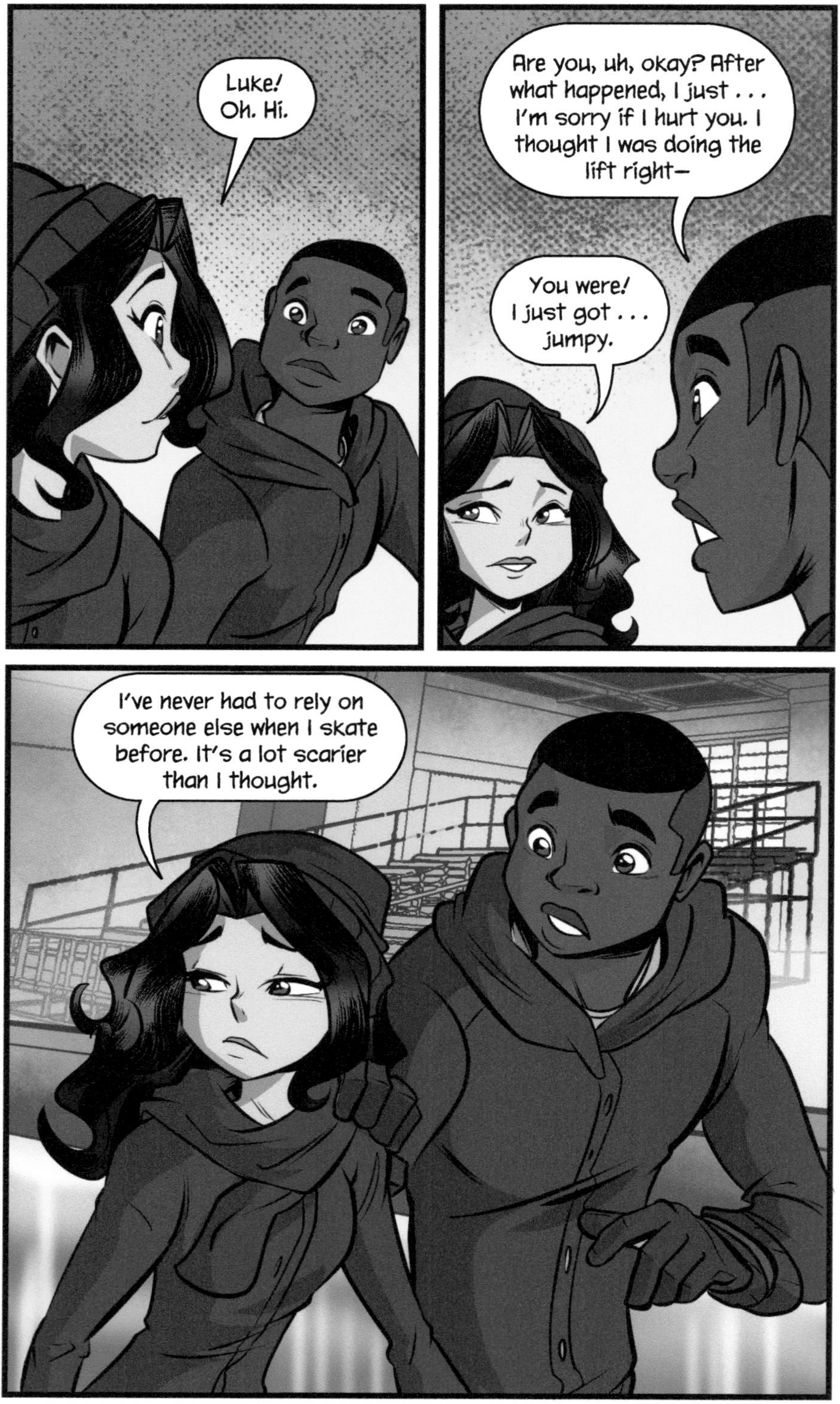
Luke! Oh. Hi.
Are you, uh, okay? After what happened, I just . . . I'm sorry if I hurt you. I thought I was doing the lift right—
You were! I just got . . . jumpy.
I've never had to rely on someone else when I skate before. It's a lot scarier than I thought.

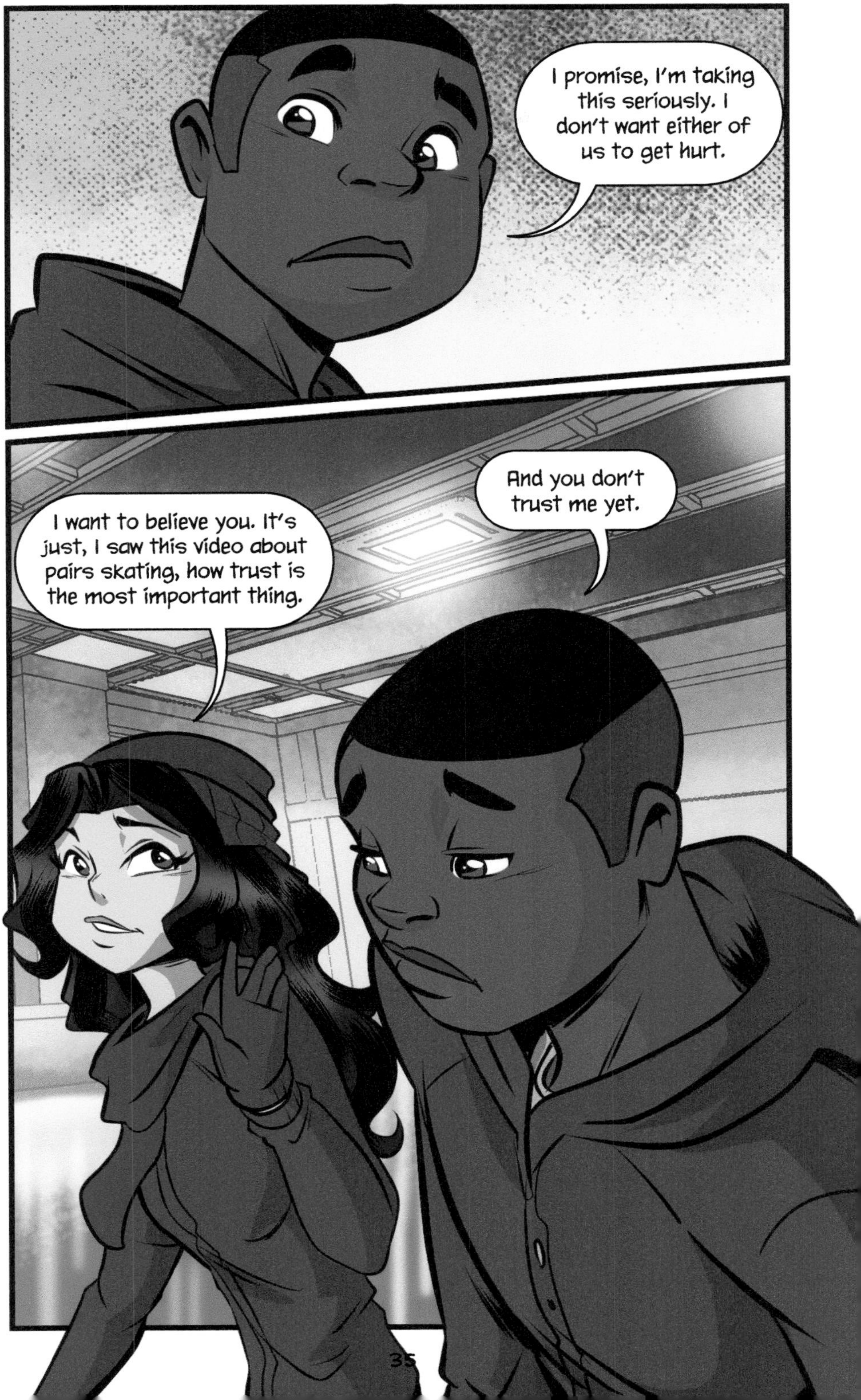
I promise, I'm taking this seriously. I don't want either of us to get hurt.
I want to believe you. It's just, I saw this video about pairs skating, how trust is the most important thing.
And you don't trust me yet.

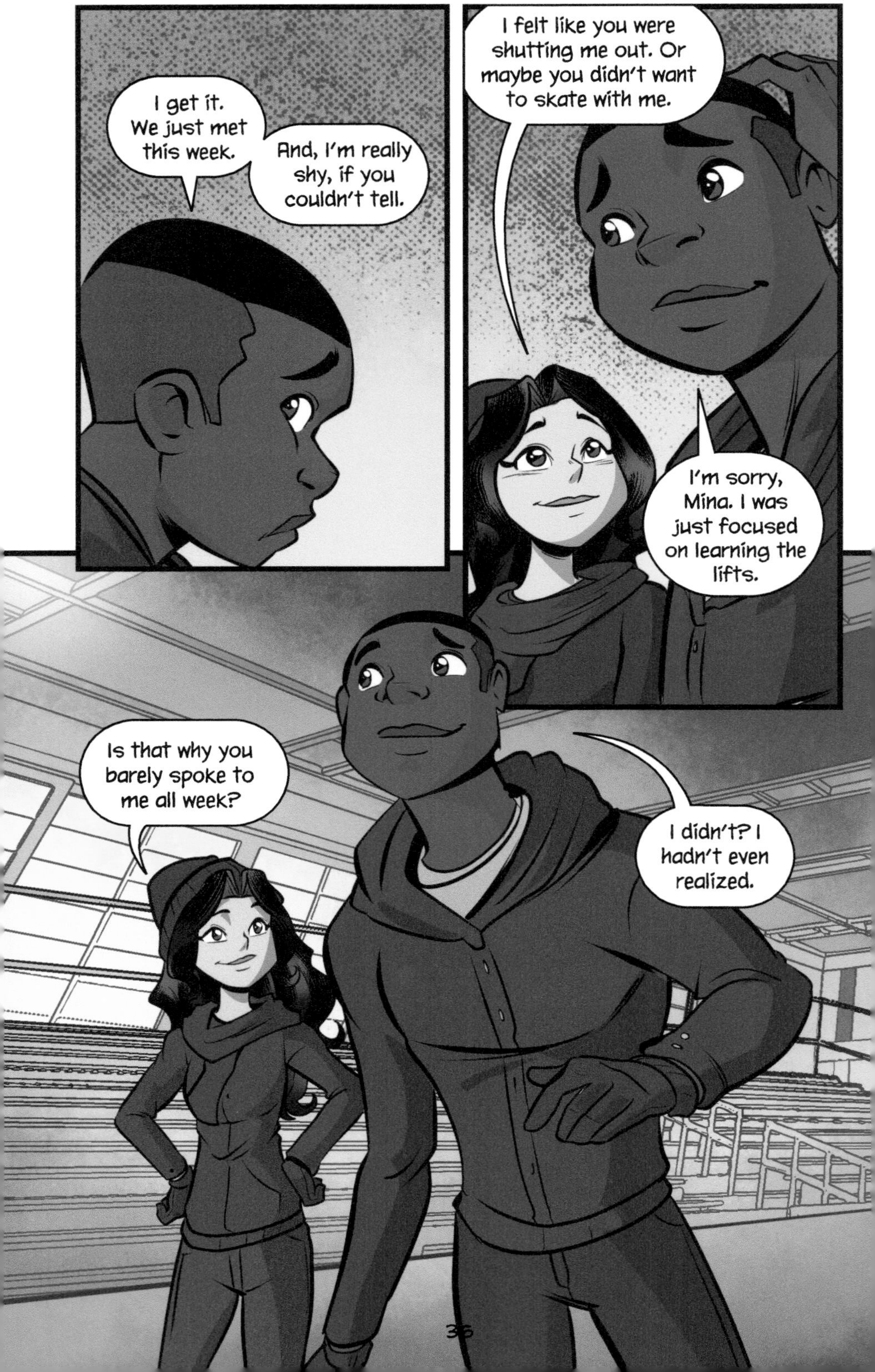
I get it. We just met this week.
And, I'm really shy, if you couldn't tell.
I felt like you were shutting me out. Or maybe you didn't want to skate with me.
I'm sorry, Mina. I was just focused on learning the lifts.
Is that why you barely spoke to me all week?
I didn't? I hadn't even realized.

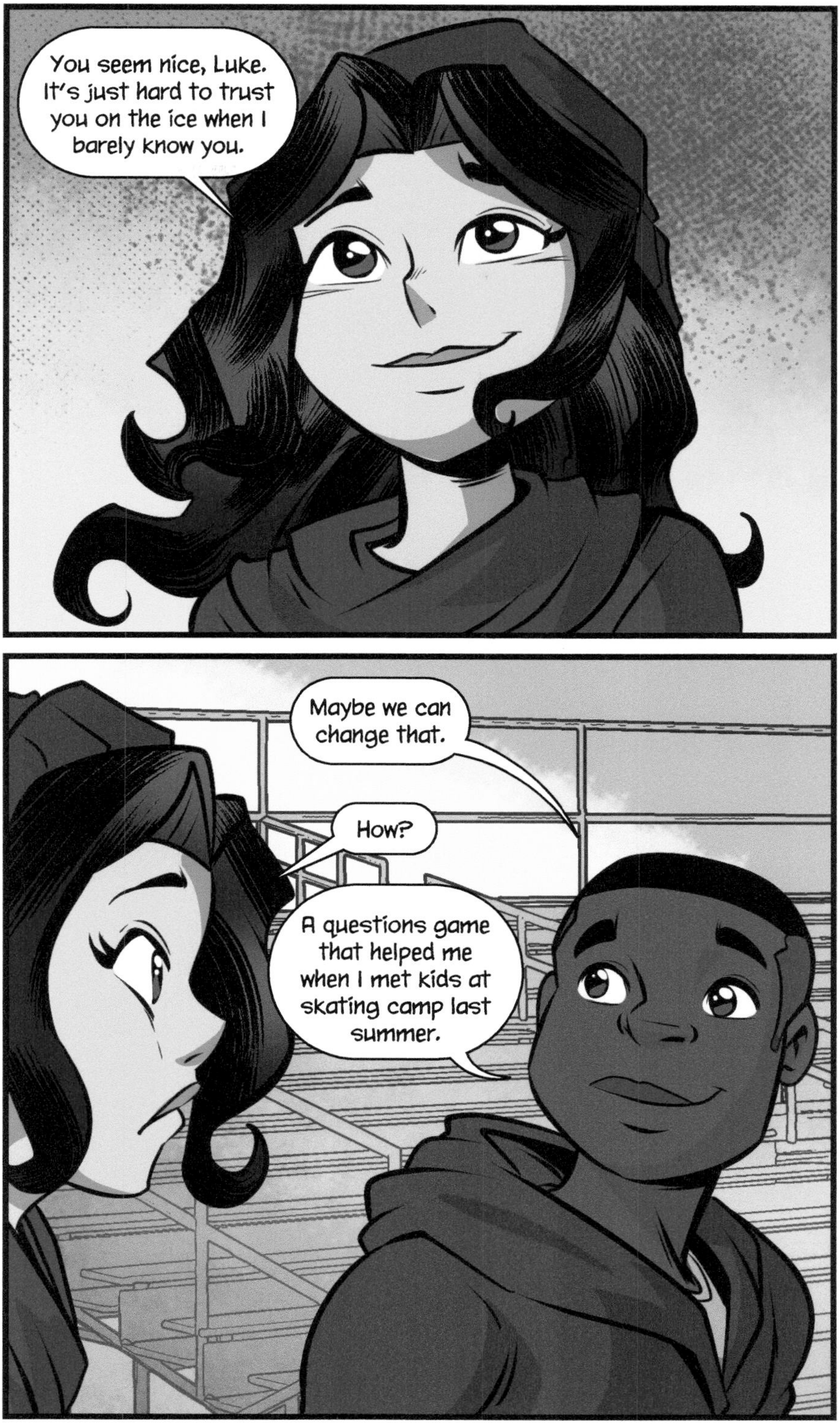
You seem nice, Luke. It's just hard to trust you on the ice when I barely know you.
Maybe we can change that.
How?
A questions game that helped me when I met kids at skating camp last summer.

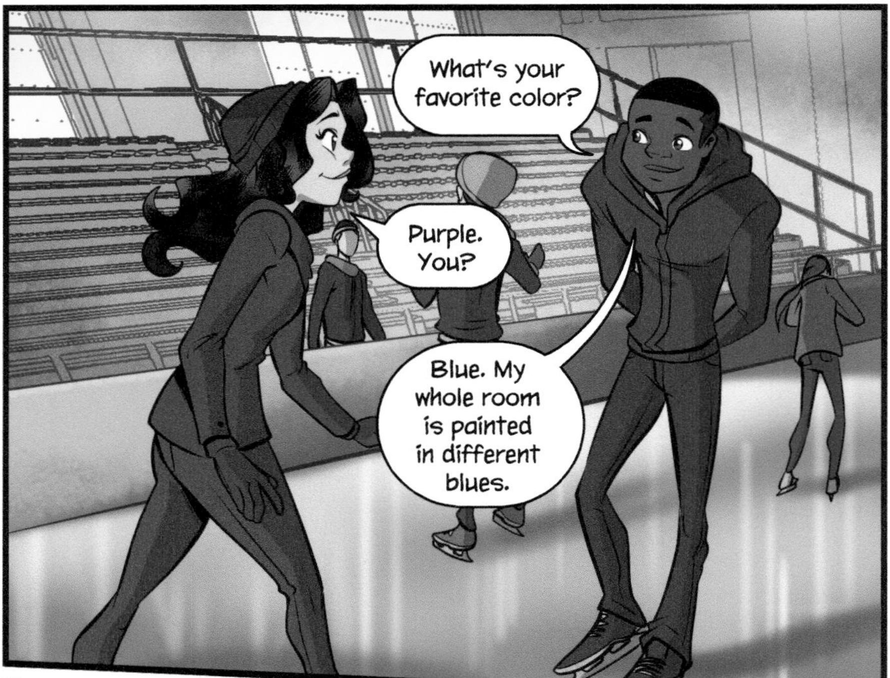
What's your favorite color?
Purple. You?
Blue. My whole room is painted in different blues.

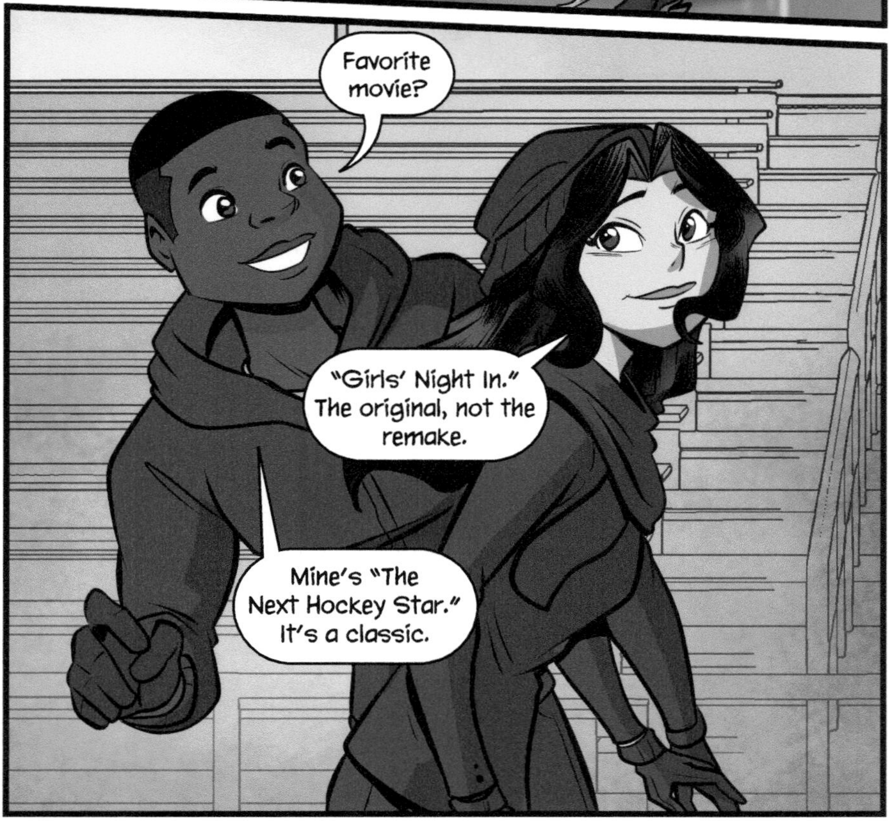
Favorite movie?
"Girls' Night In." The original, not the remake.
Mine's "The Next Hockey Star." It's a classic.

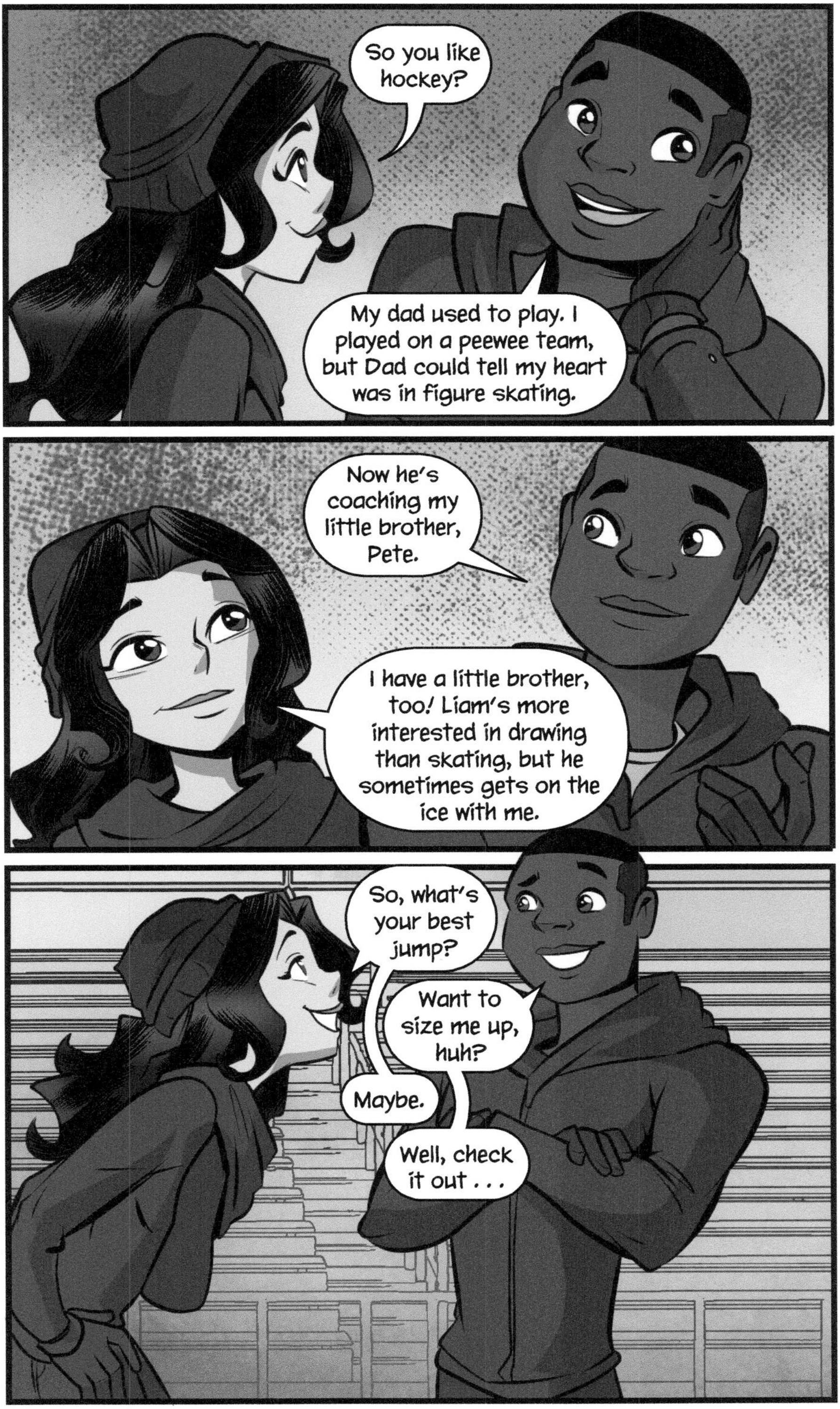
So you like hockey?
My dad used to play. I played on a peewee team, but Dad could tell my heart was in figure skating.
Now he's coaching my little brother, Pete.
I have a little brother, too! Liam's more interested in drawing than skating, but he sometimes gets on the ice with me.
So, what's your best jump?
Want to size me up, huh?
Maybe.
Well, check it out . . .

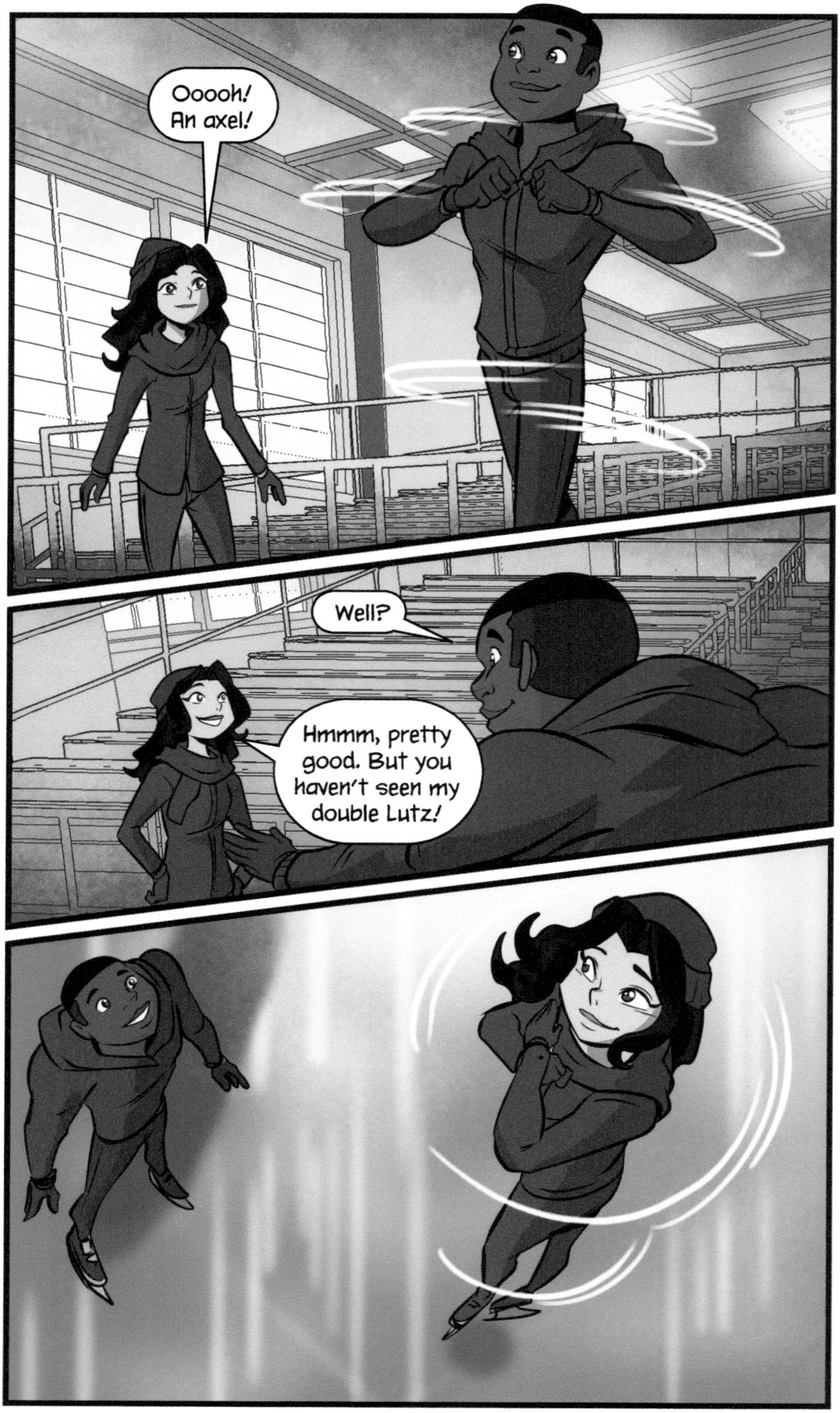
Ooooh! An axel!
Well?
Hmmm, pretty good. But you haven't seen my double Lutz!

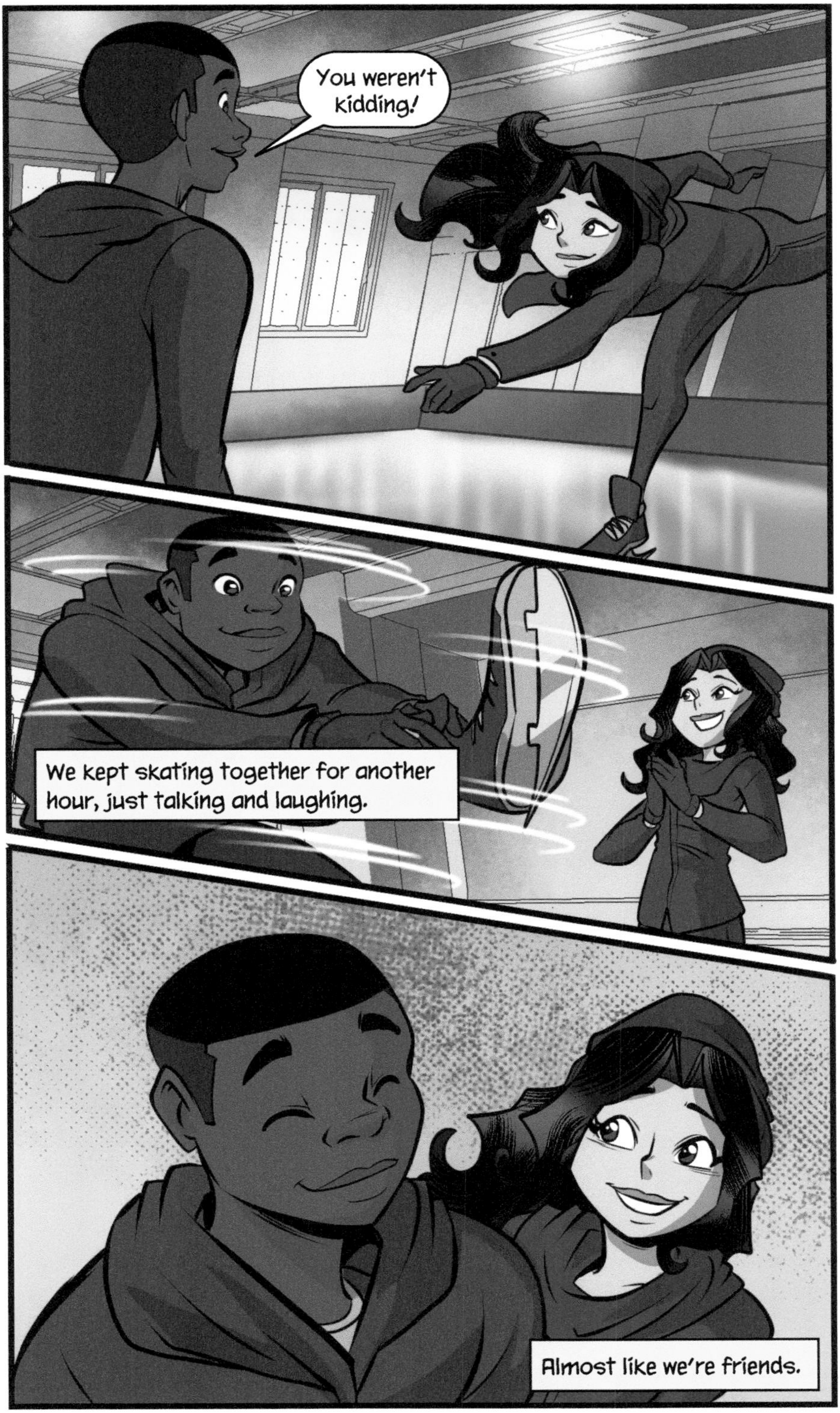
You weren't kidding!
We kept skating together for another hour, just talking and laughing.
Almost like we're friends.

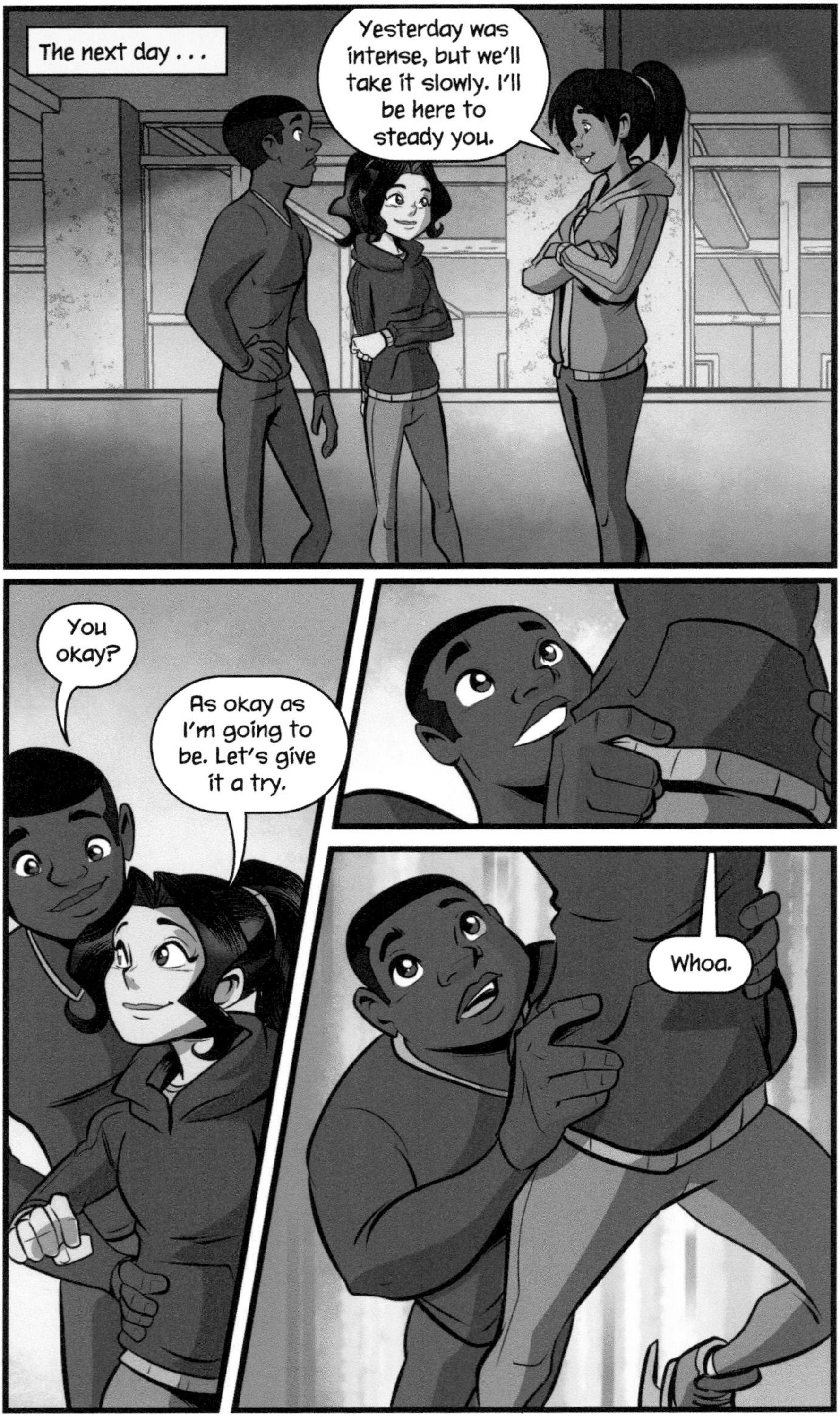

The next day . . .
Yesterday was intense, but we'll take it slowly. I'll be here to steady you.
You okay?
As okay as I'm going to be. Let's give it a try.
Whoa.

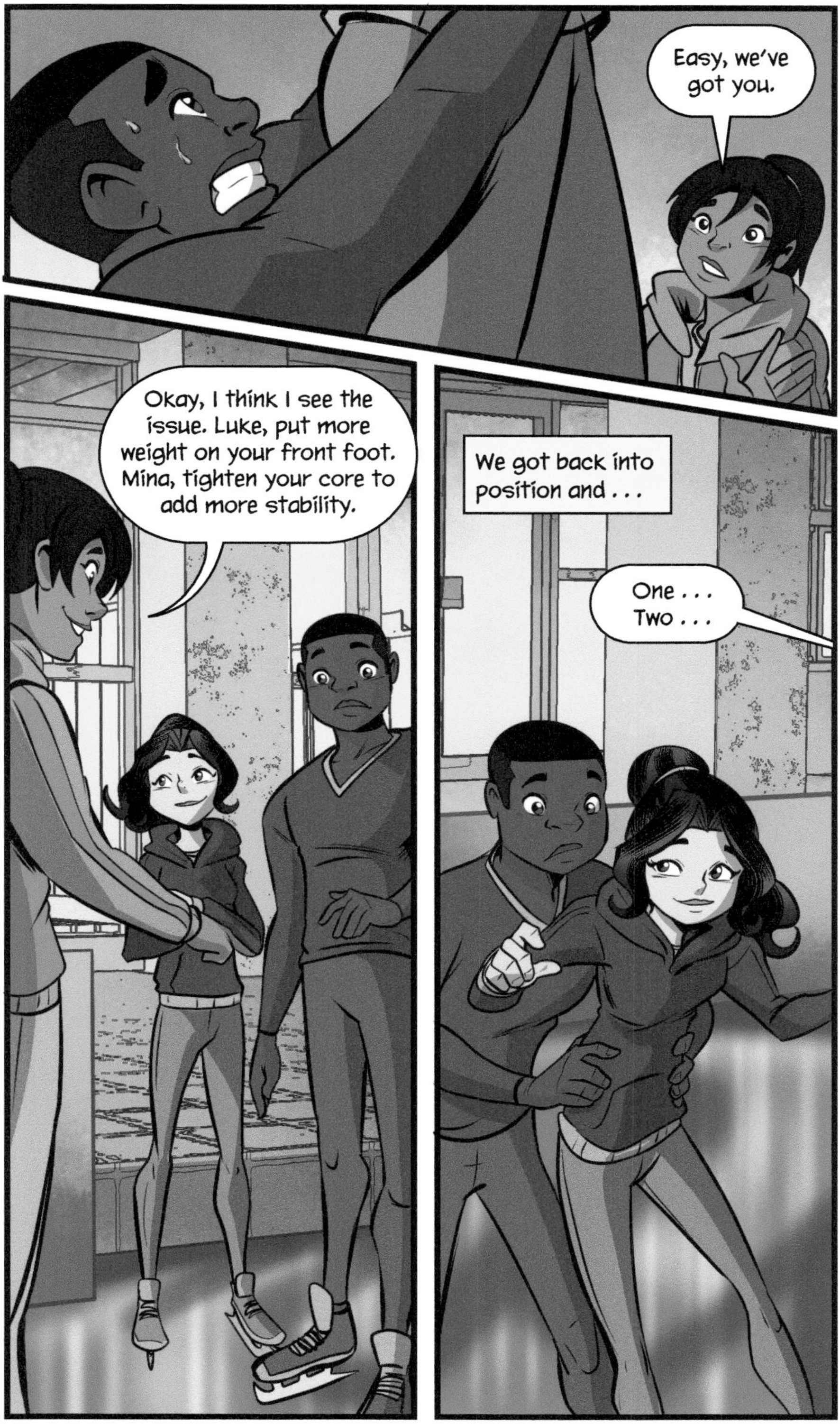
Easy, we've got you.
Okay, I think I see the issue. Luke, put more weight on your front foot. Mina, tighten your core to add more stability.
We got back into position and . . .
One . . .
Two . . .

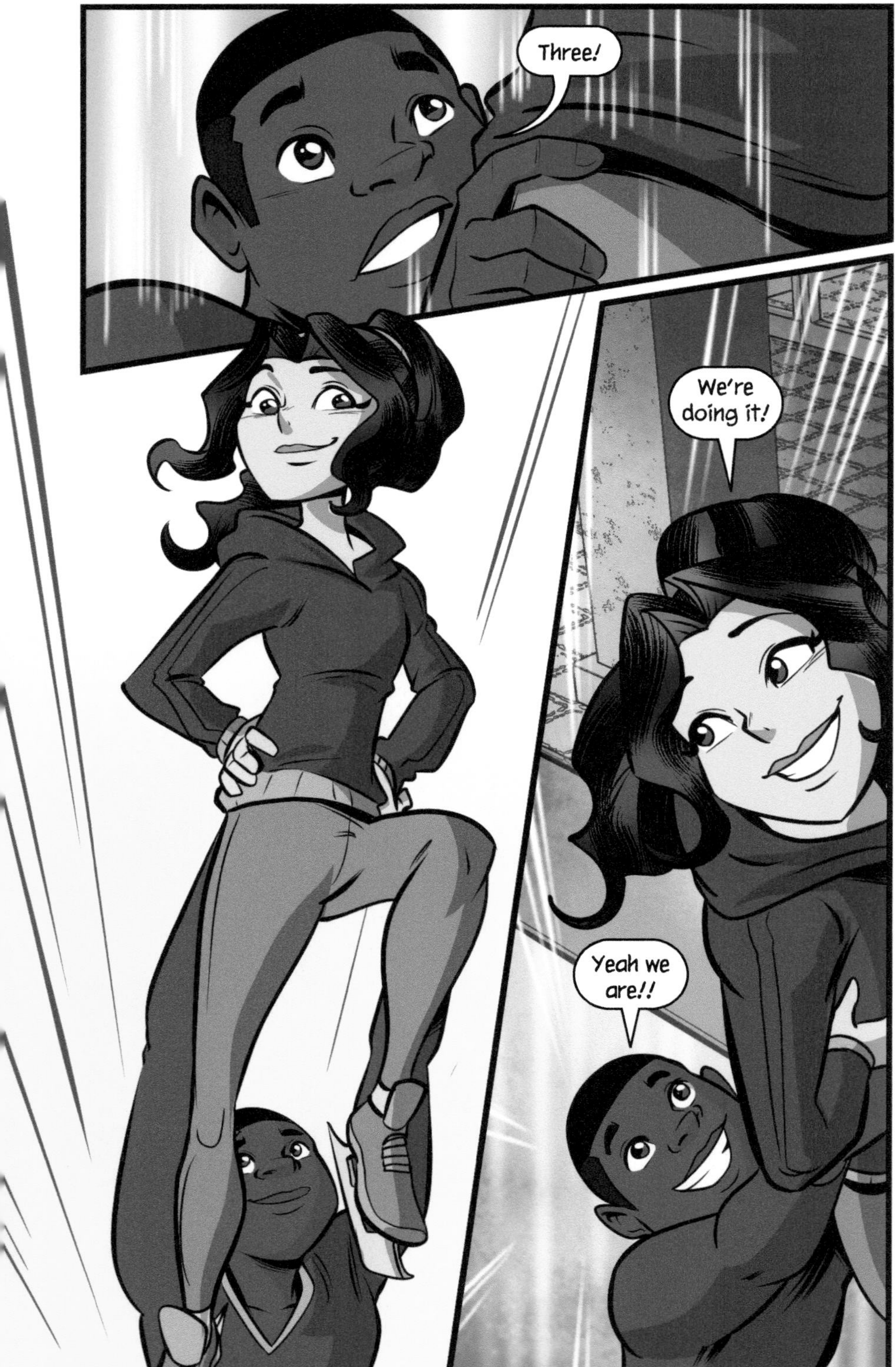
Three!
We're doing it!
Yeah we are!!

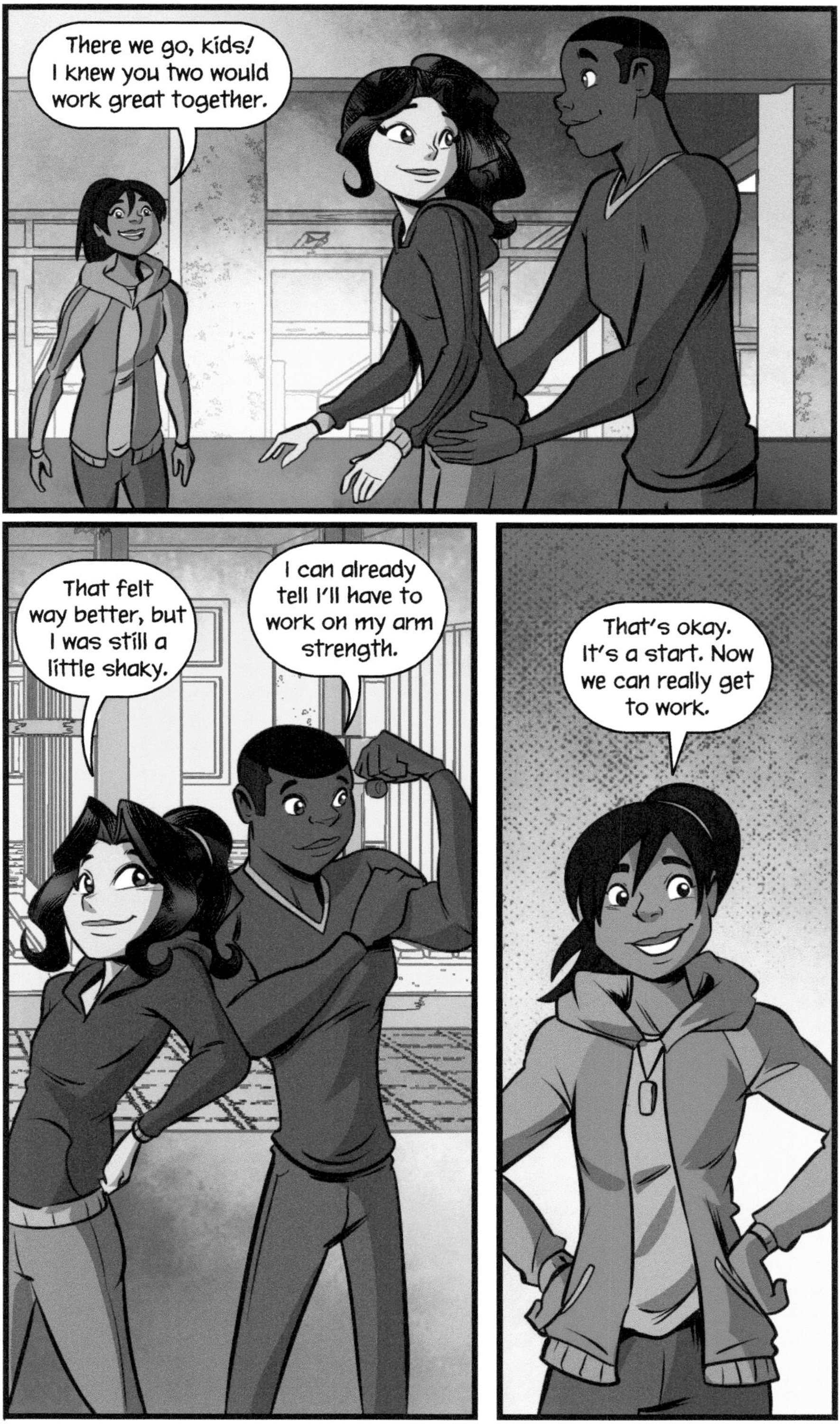

There we go, kids! I knew you two would work great together.
That felt way better, but I was still a little shaky.
I can already tell I'll have to work on my arm strength.
That's okay. It's a start. Now we can really get to work.

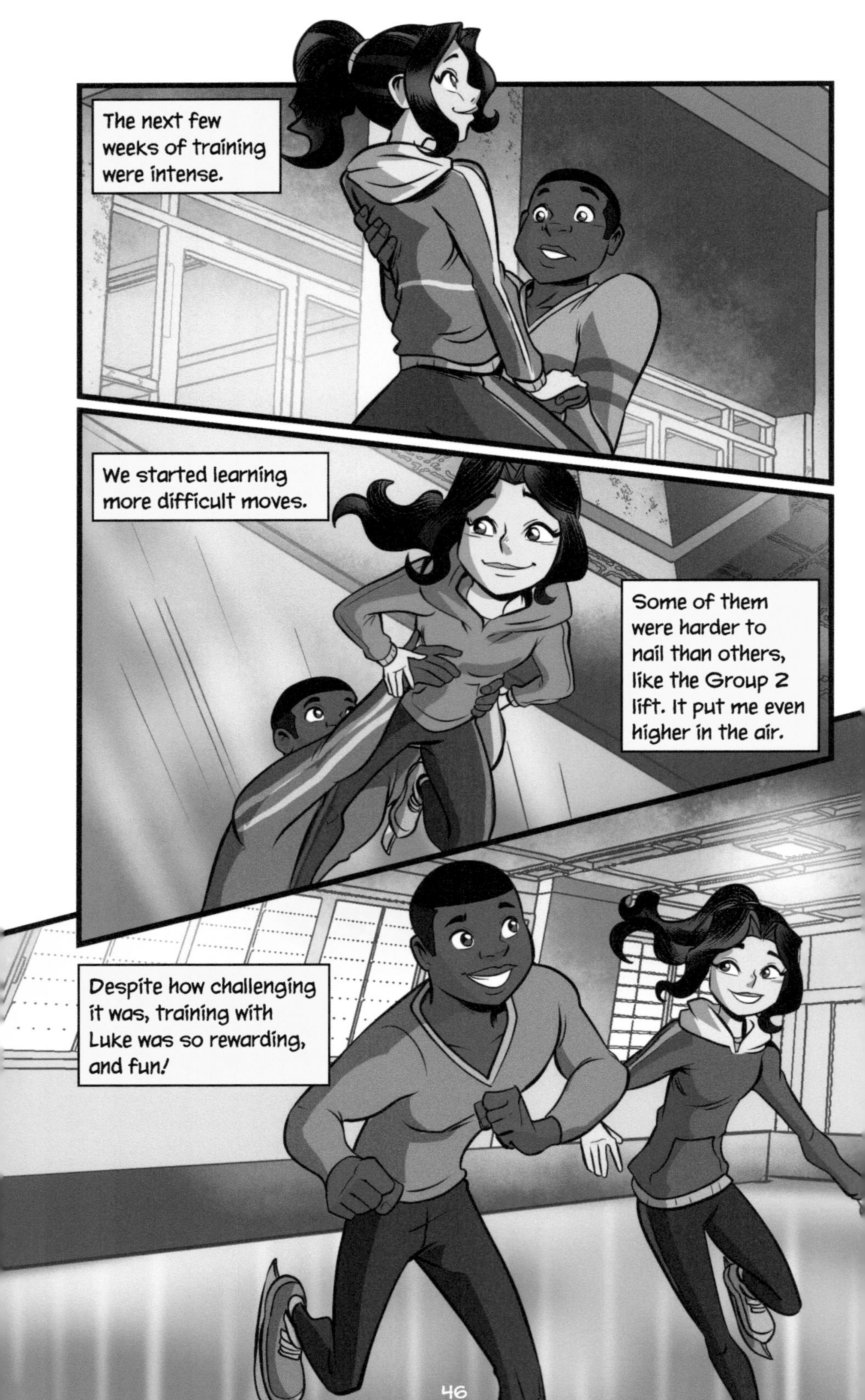
The next few weeks of training were intense.
We started learning more difficult moves.
Some of them were harder to nail than others, like the Group 2 lift. It put me even higher in the air.
Despite how challenging it was, training with Luke was so rewarding, and fun!

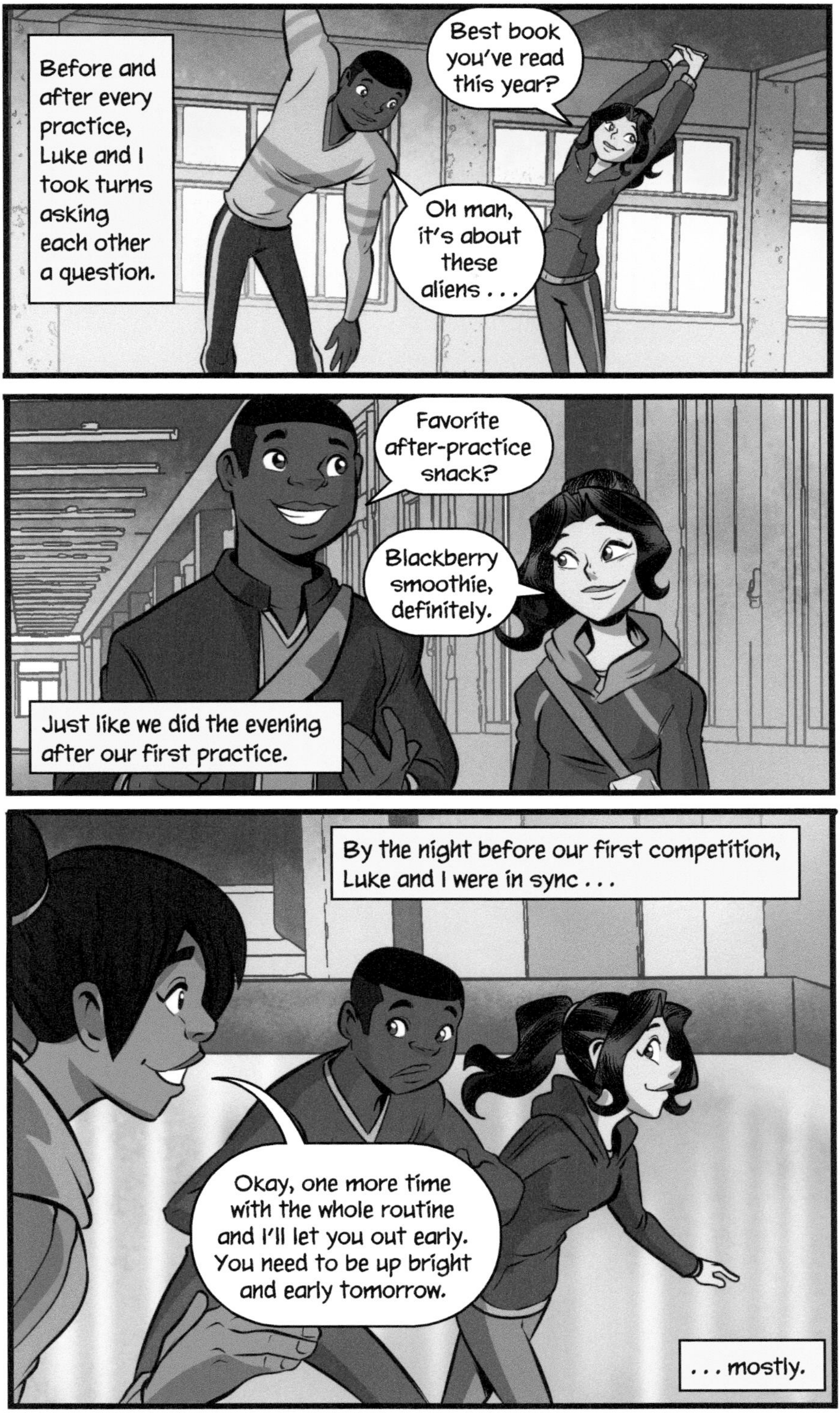
Before and after every practice, Luke and I took turns asking each other a question.
Best book you've read this year?
Oh man, it's about these aliens . . .
Favorite after-practice snack?
Blackberry smoothie, definitely.
Just like we did the evening after our first practice.
By the night before our first competition, Luke and I were in sync . . .
Okay, one more time with the whole routine and I'll let you out early. You need to be up bright and early tomorrow.
. . . mostly.

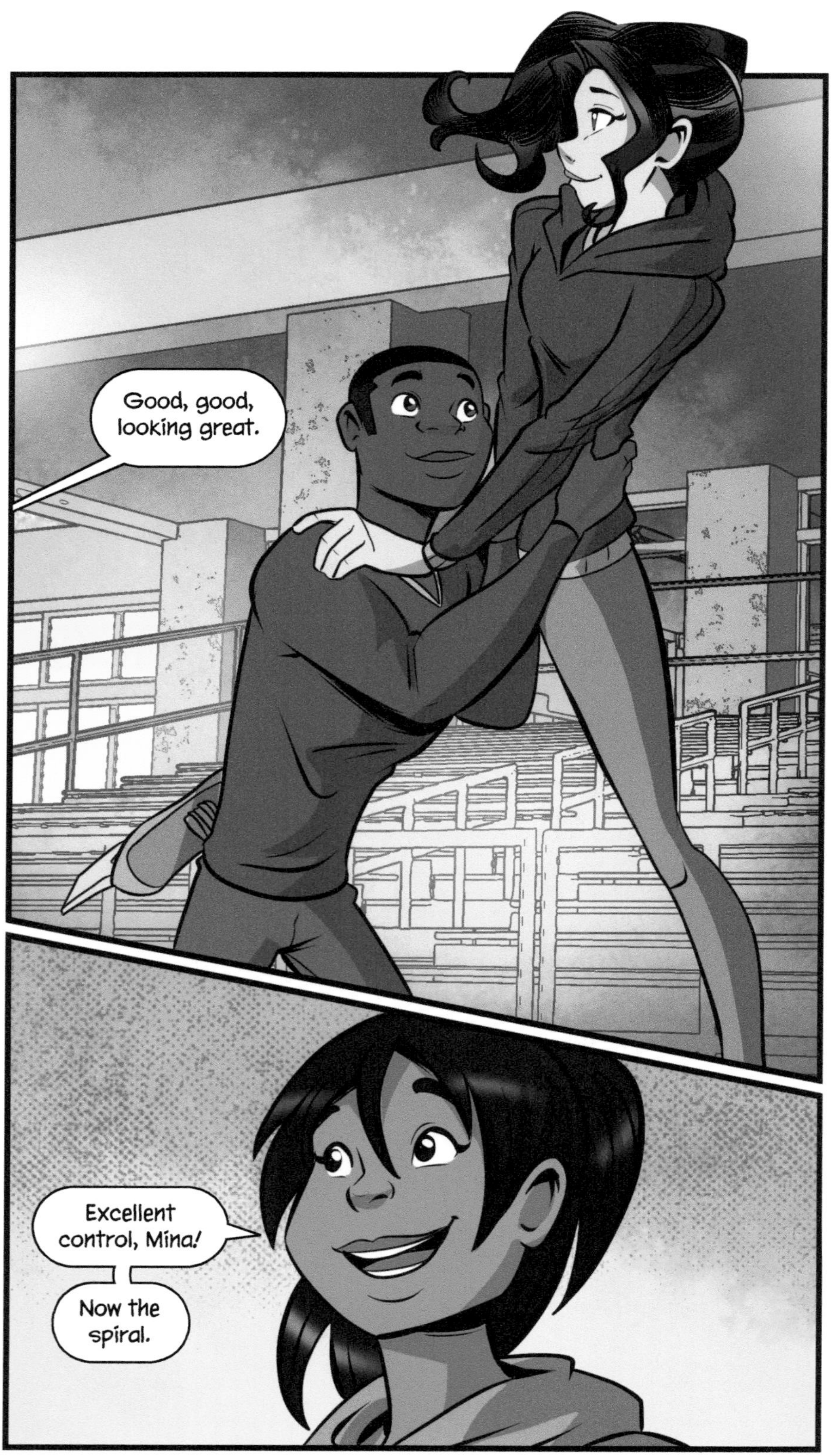
Good, good, looking great.
Excellent control, Mina!
Now the spiral.

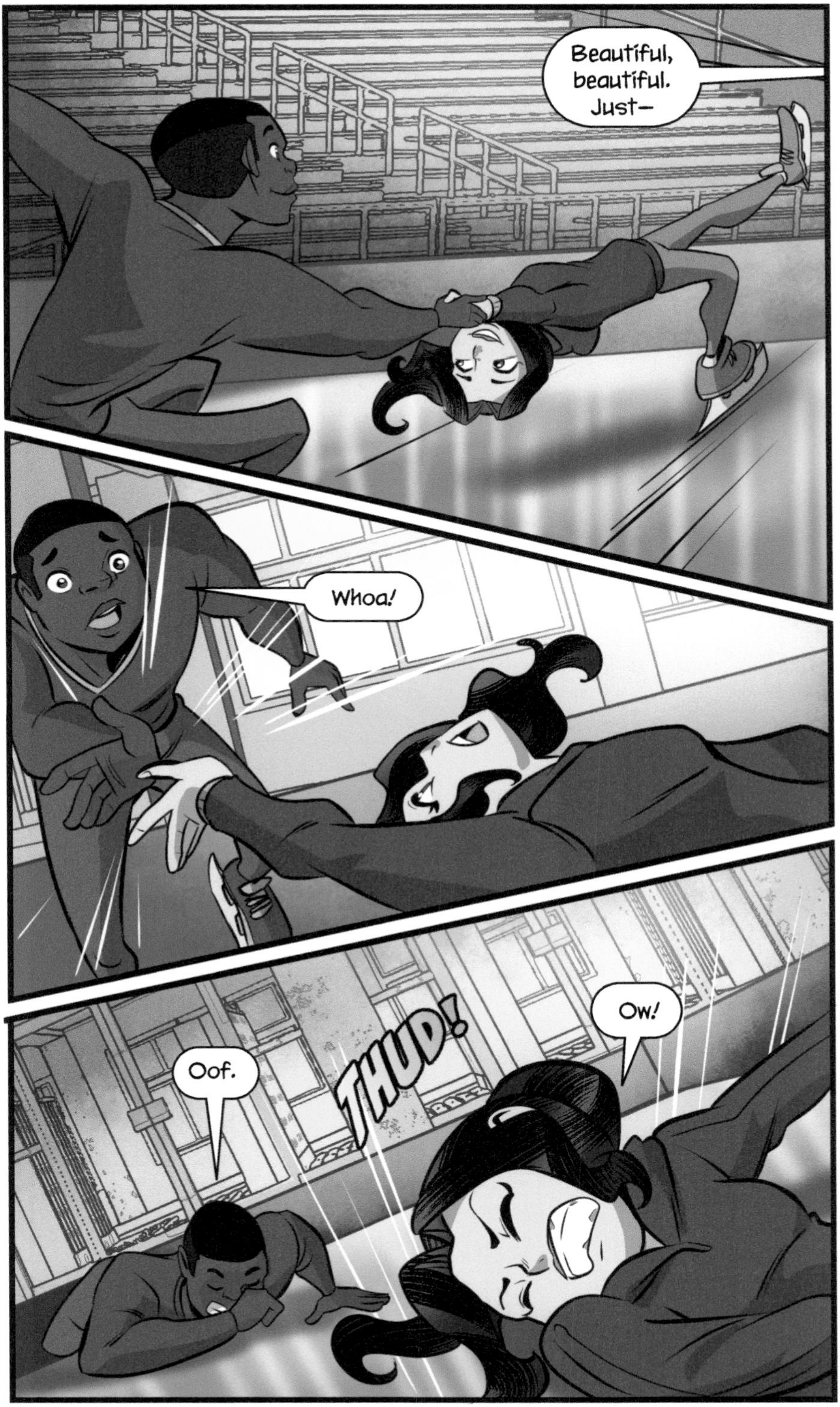
Beautiful, beautiful. Just—
Whoa!
THUD!
Ow!
Oof.

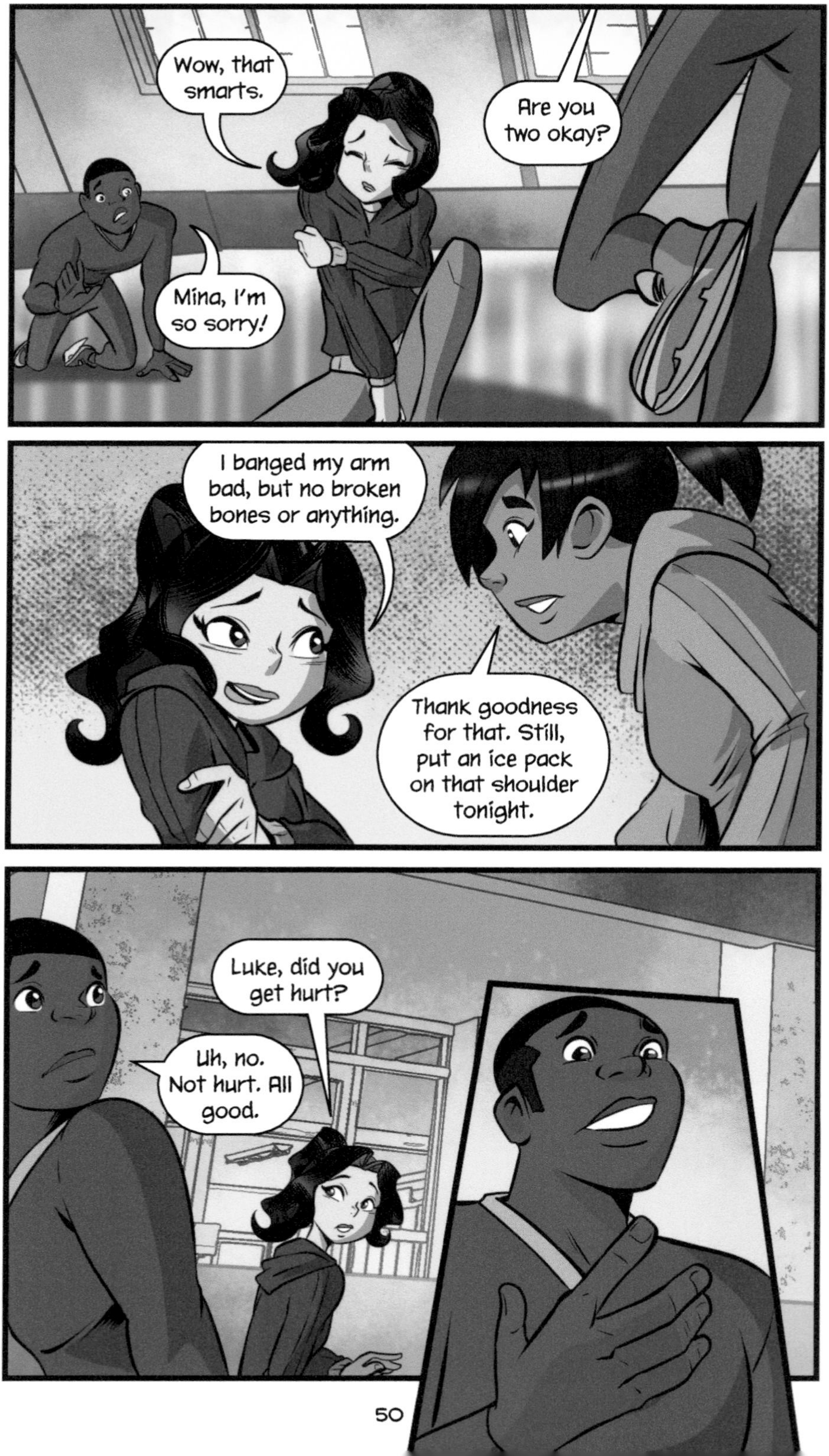

Wow, that smarts.
Are you two okay?
Mina, I'm so sorry!
I banged my arm bad, but no broken bones or anything.
Thank goodness for that. Still, put an ice pack on that shoulder tonight.
Luke, did you get hurt?
Uh, no. Not hurt. All good.

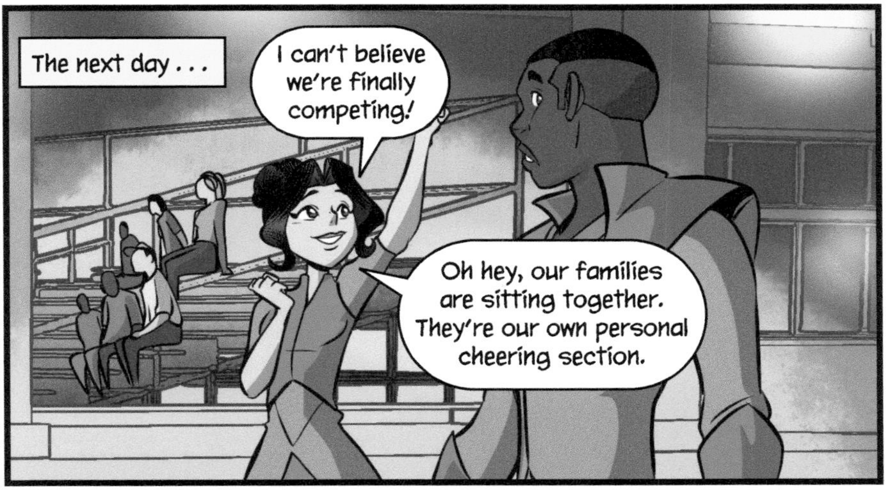
The next day . . .
I can't believe we're finally competing!
Oh hey, our families are sitting together. They're our own personal cheering section.

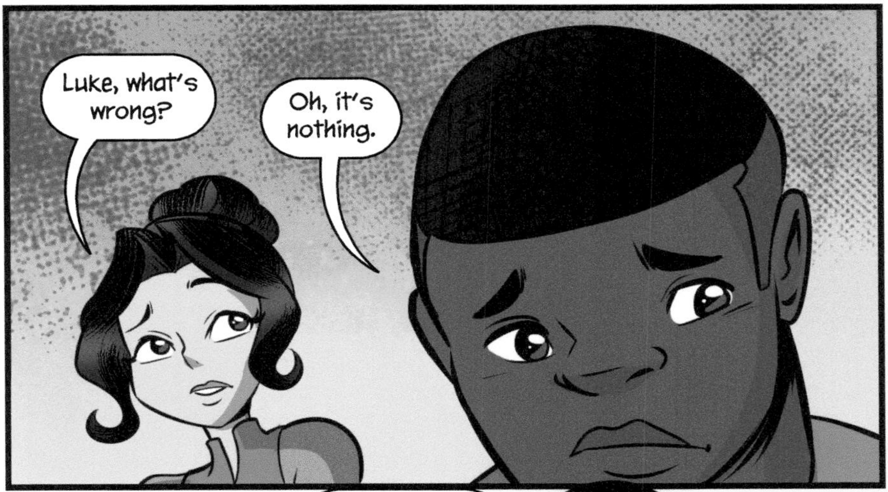
Luke, what's wrong?
Oh, it's nothing.

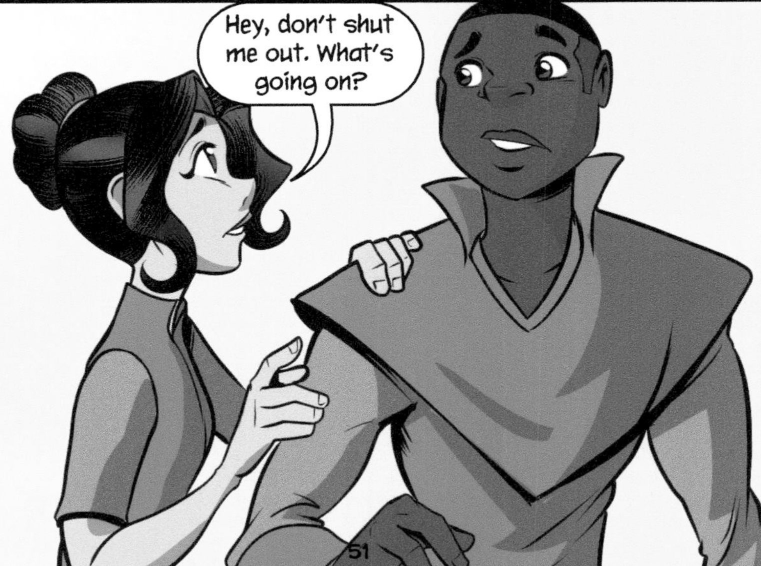
Hey, don't shut me out. What's going on?

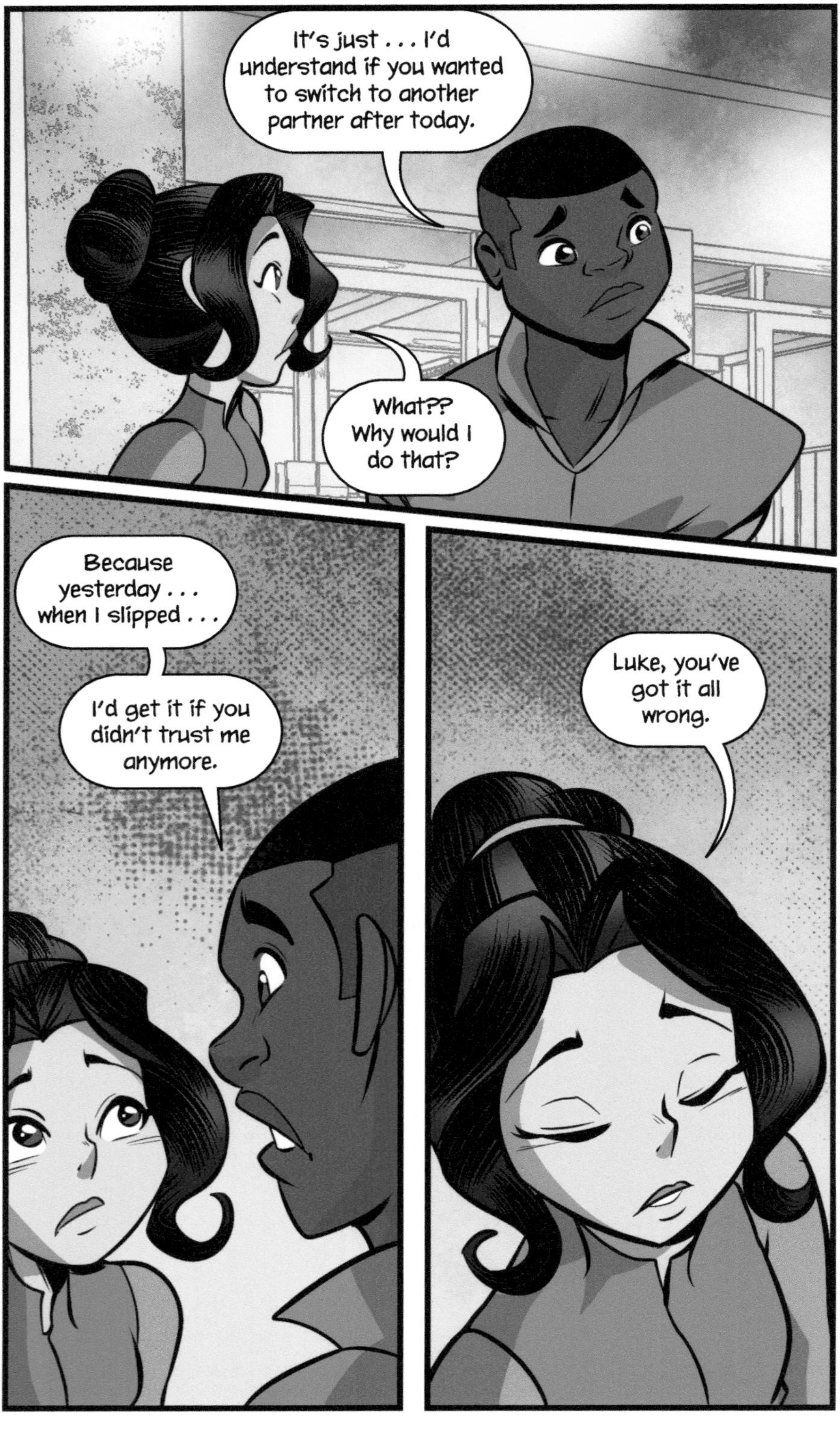
It's just . . . I'd understand if you wanted to switch to another partner after today.
What?? Why would I do that?
Because yesterday . . . when I slipped . . .
I'd get it if you didn't trust me anymore.
Luke, you've got it all wrong.

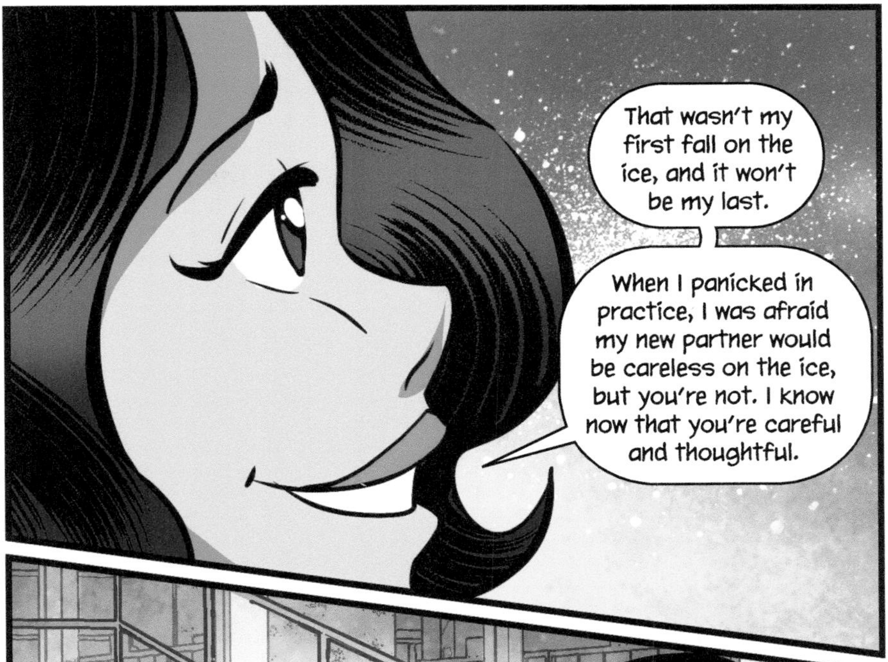
That wasn't my first fall on the ice, and it won't be my last.
When I panicked in practice, I was afraid my new partner would be careless on the ice, but you're not. I know now that you're careful and thoughtful.

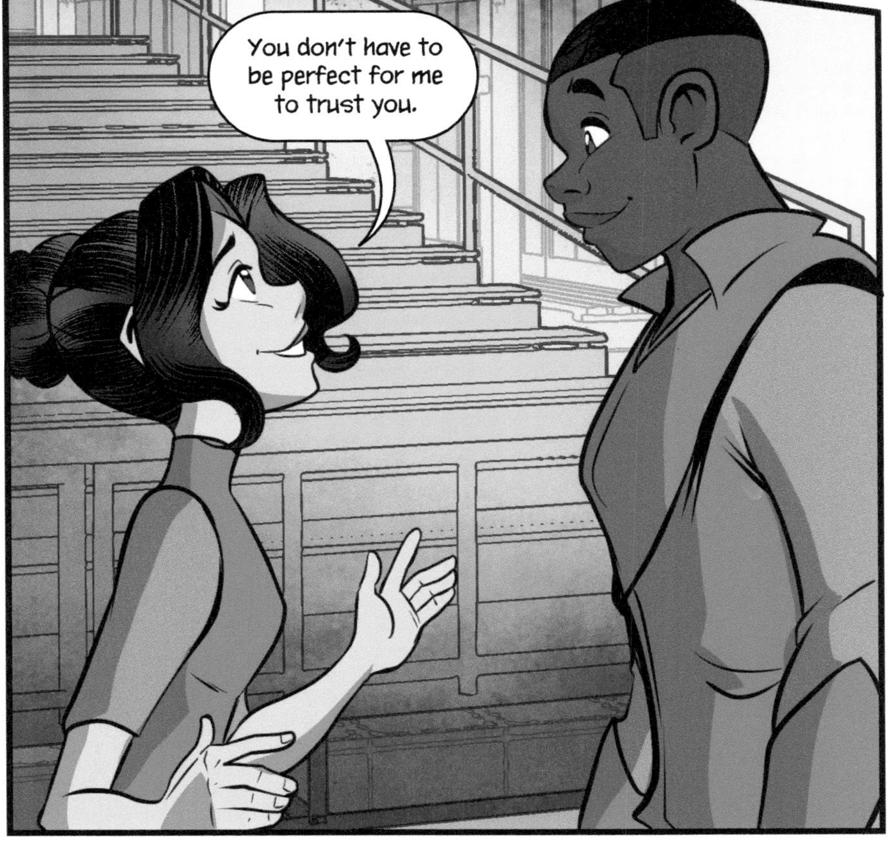
You don't have to be perfect for me to trust you.

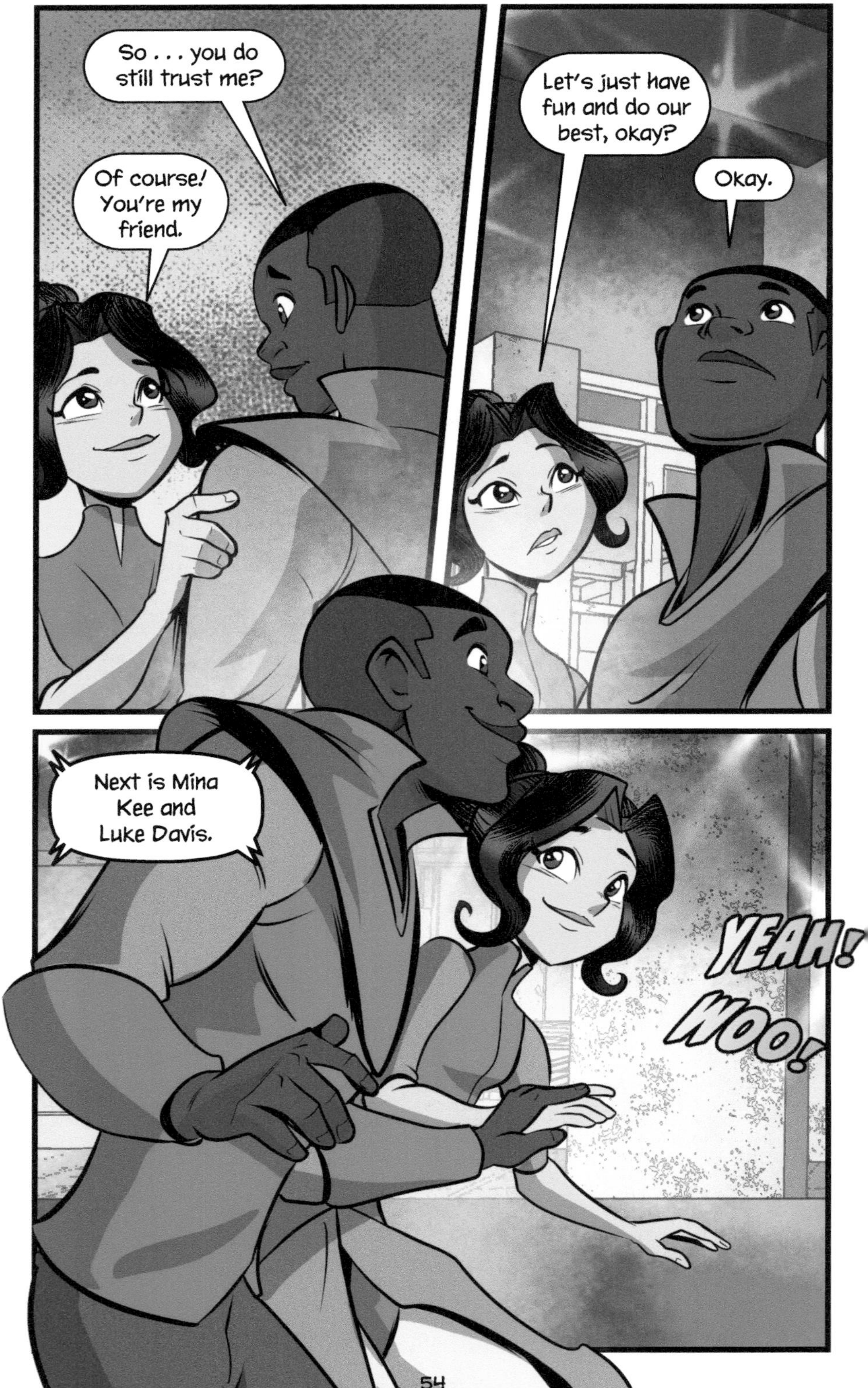
So . . . you do still trust me?
Of course! You're my friend.
Let's just have fun and do our best, okay?
Okay.
Next is Mina Kee and Luke Davis.
YEAH!
WOO!

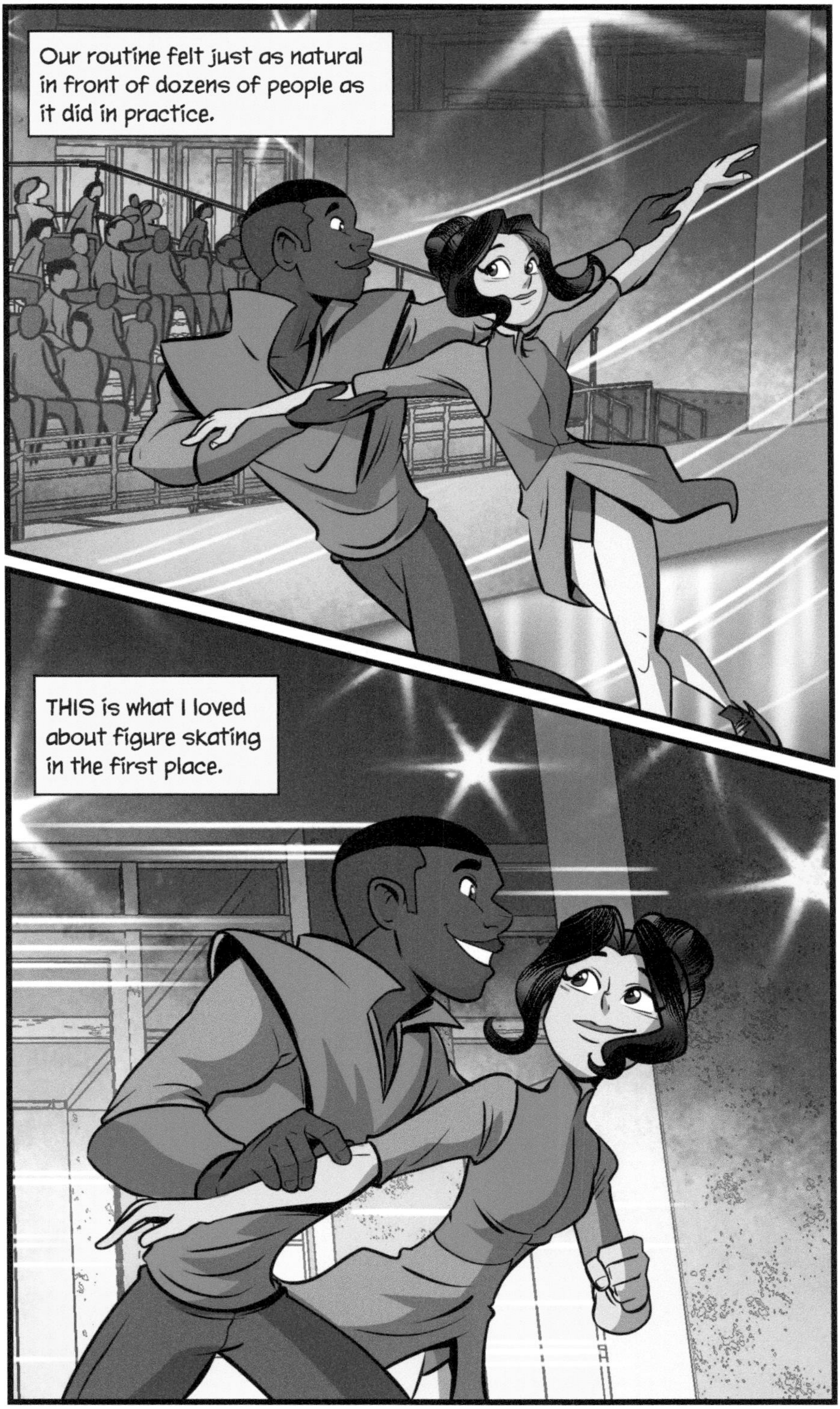
Our routine felt just as natural in front of dozens of people as it did in practice.
THIS is what I loved about figure skating in the first place.

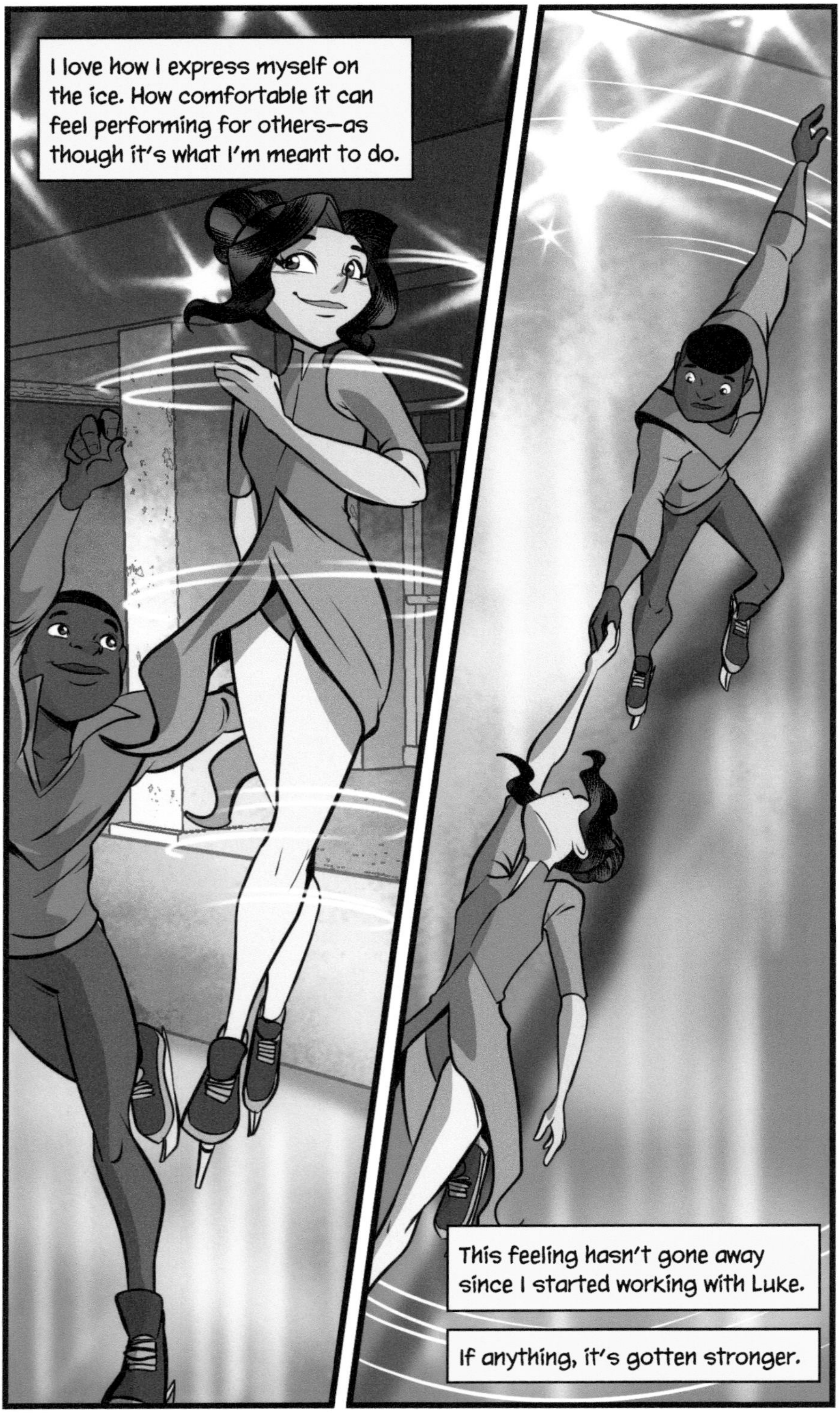
I love how I express myself on the ice. How comfortable it can feel performing for others—as though it's what I'm meant to do.
This feeling hasn't gone away since I started working with Luke.
If anything, it's gotten stronger.

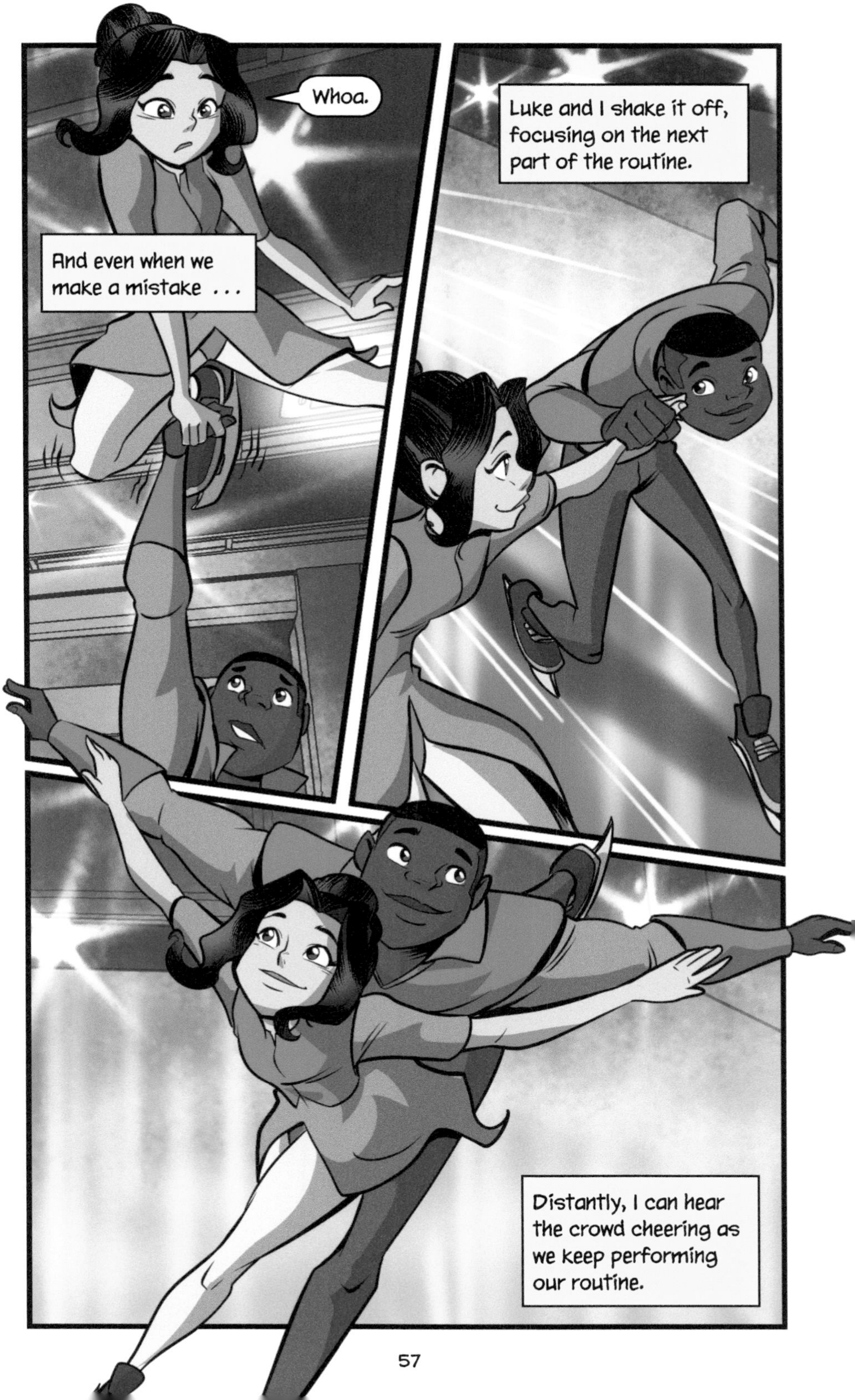
Whoa.
And even when we make a mistake . . .
Luke and I shake it off, focusing on the next part of the routine.
Distantly, I can hear the crowd cheering as we keep performing our routine.

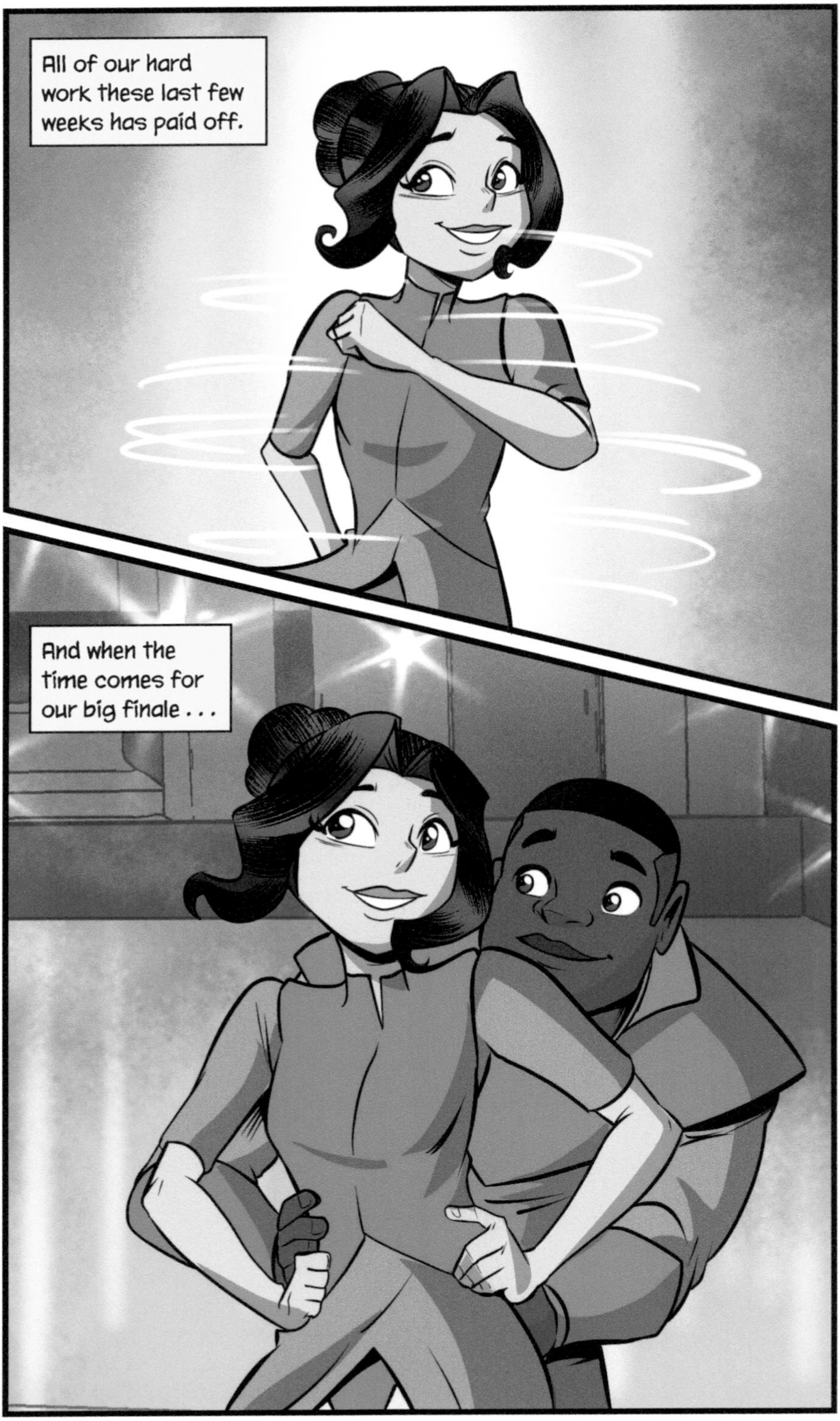
All of our hard work these last few weeks has paid off.
And when the time comes for our big finale . . .

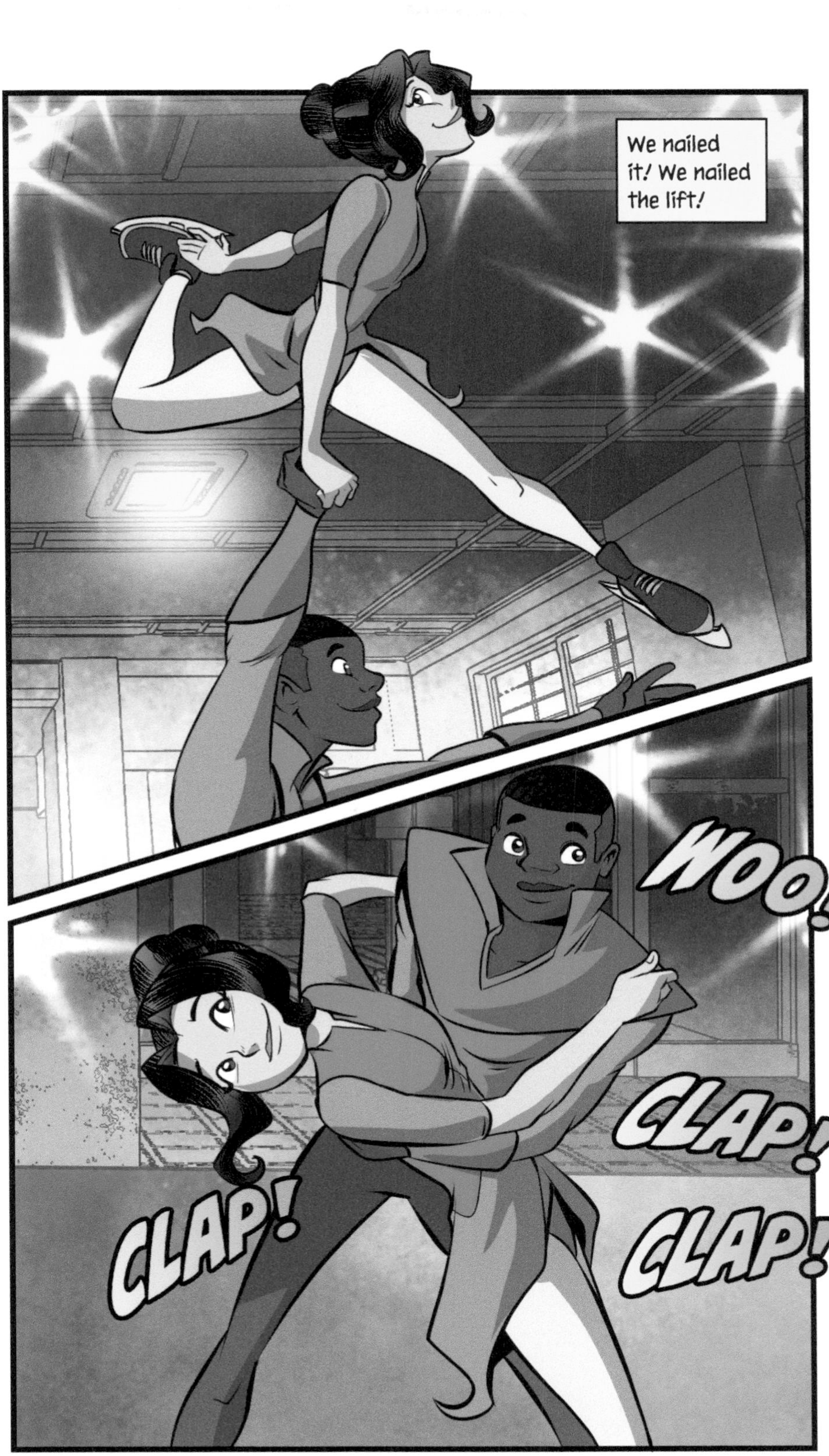
We nailed it! We nailed the lift!
WOO!
CLAP!
CLAP!
CLAP!

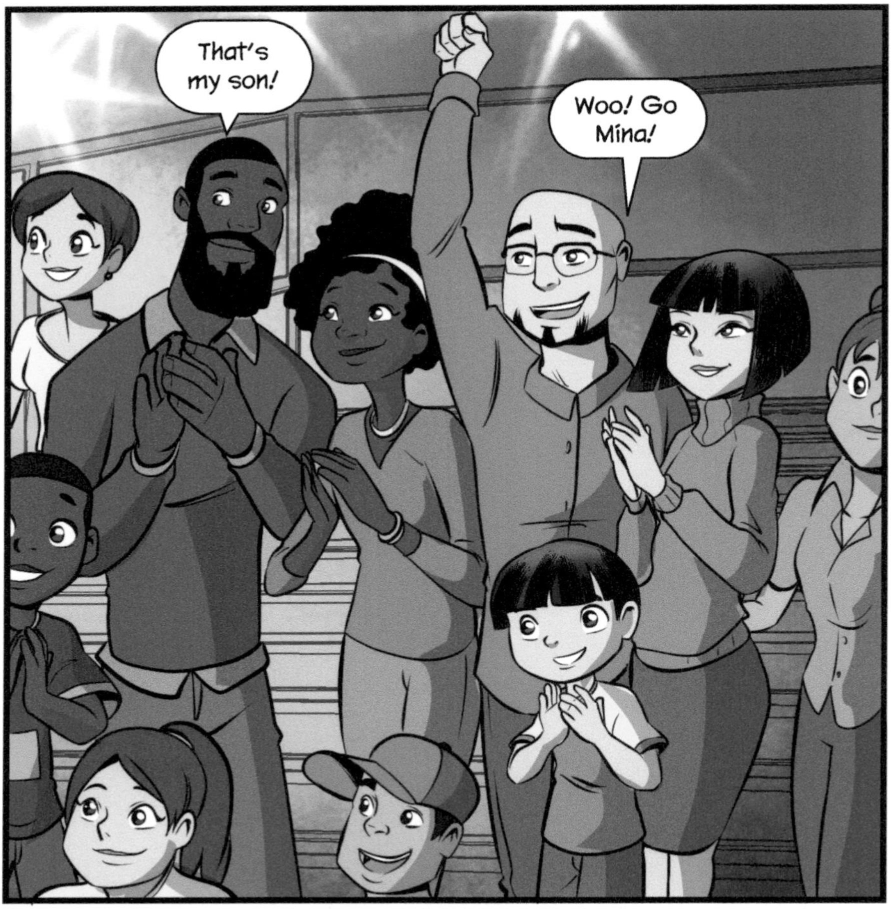
That's my son!
Woo! Go Mina!

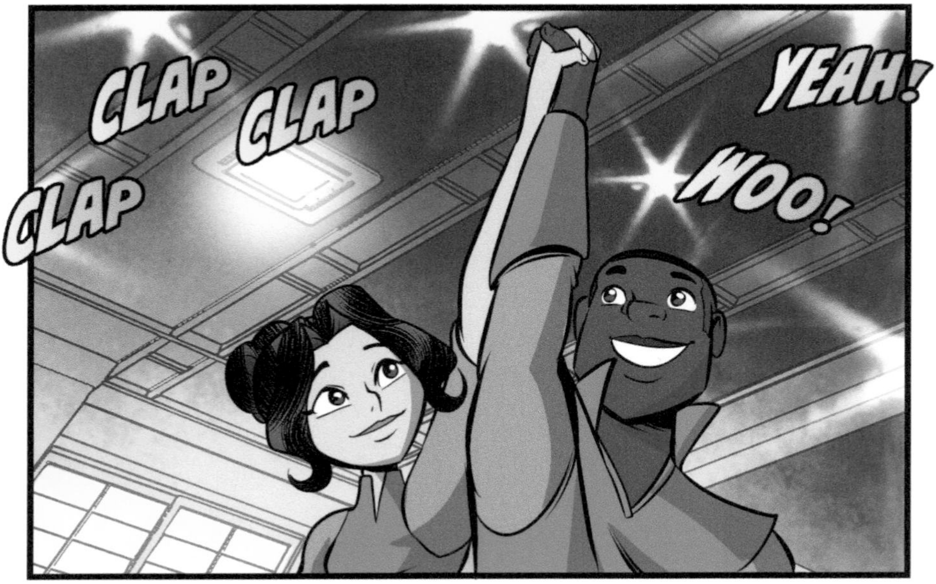
CLAP
CLAP
CLAP
YEAH!
WOO!

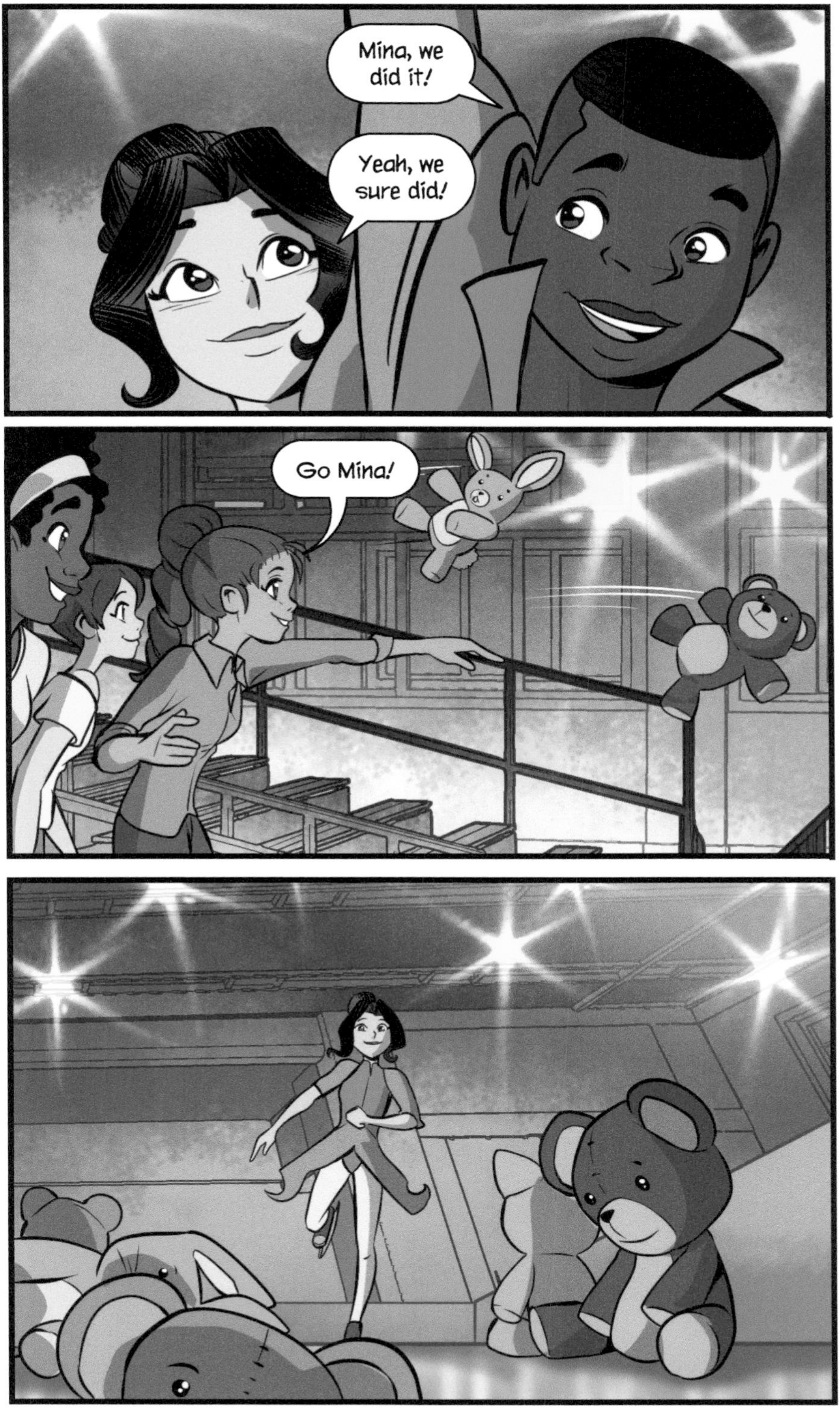
Mina, we did it!
Yeah, we sure did!
Go Mina!

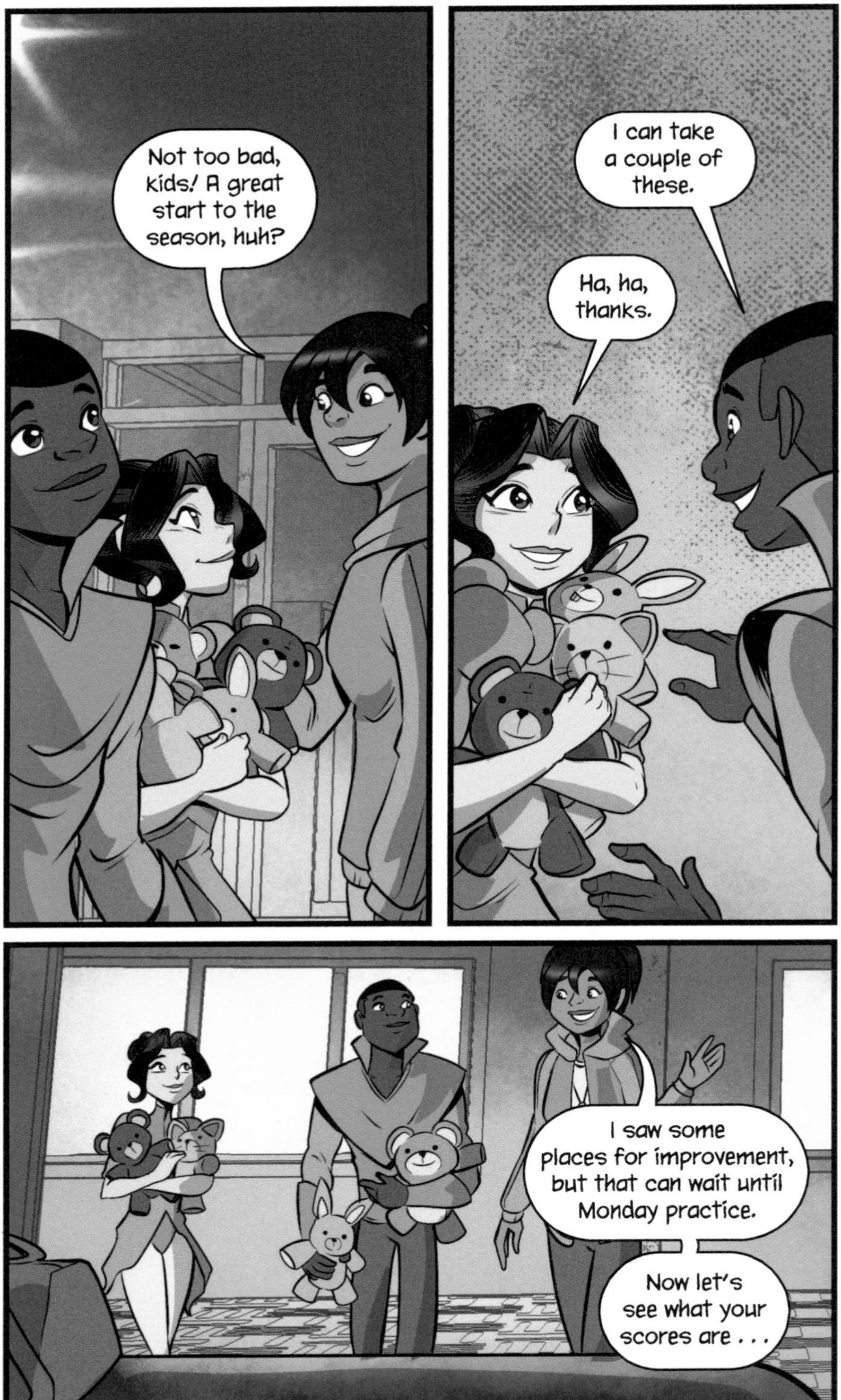
Not too bad, kids! A great start to the season, huh?
Ha, ha, thanks.
I can take a couple of these.
I saw some places for improvement, but that can wait until Monday practice.
Now let's see what your scores are . . .

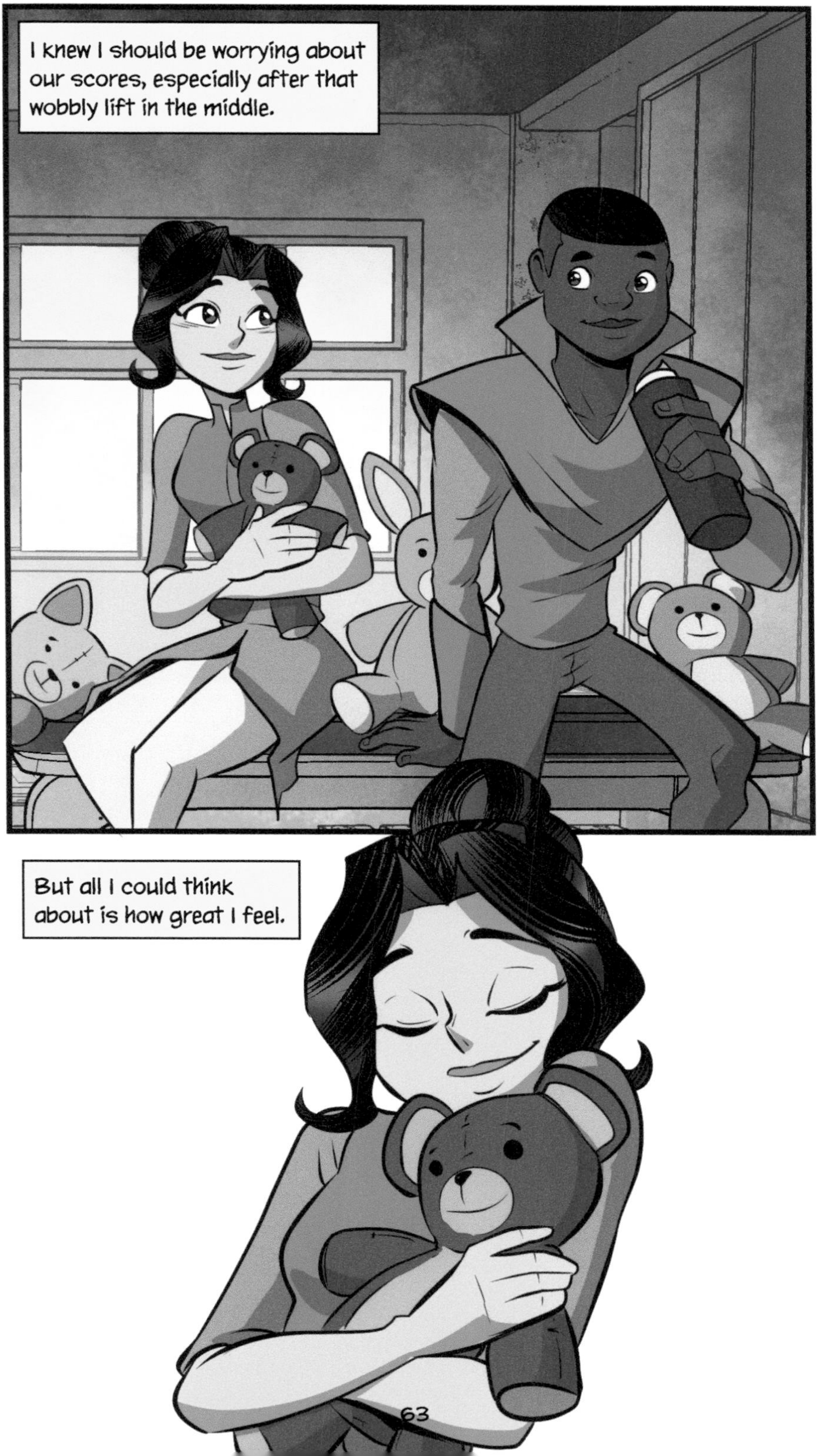
I knew I should be worrying about our scores, especially after that wobbly lift in the middle.
But all I could think about is how great I feel.

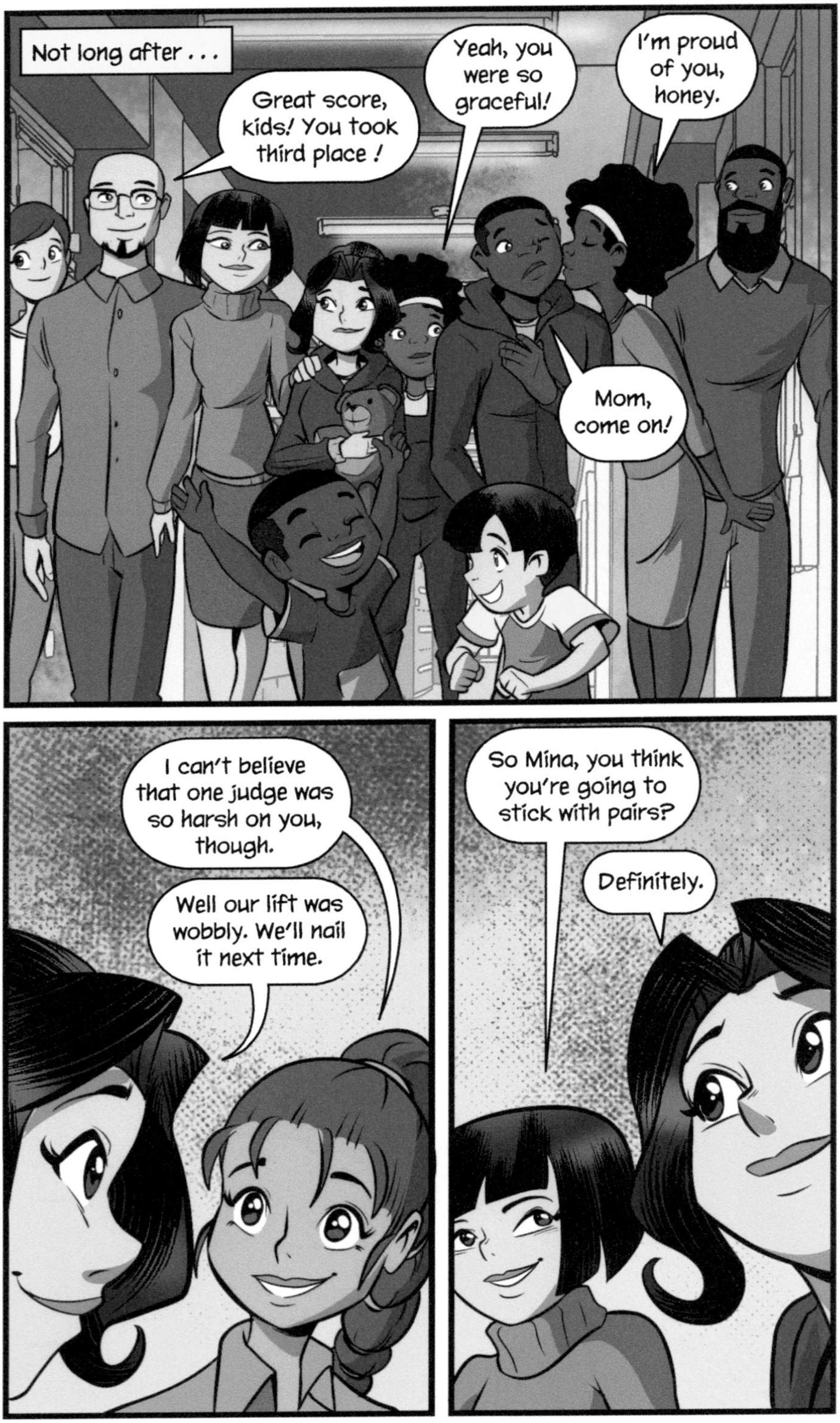
Not long after . . .
Great score, kids! You took third place!
Yeah, you were so graceful!
I'm proud of you, honey.
Mom, come on!
I can't believe that one judge was so harsh on you, though.
Well our lift was wobbly. We'll nail it next time.
So Mina, you think you're going to stick with pairs?
Definitely.

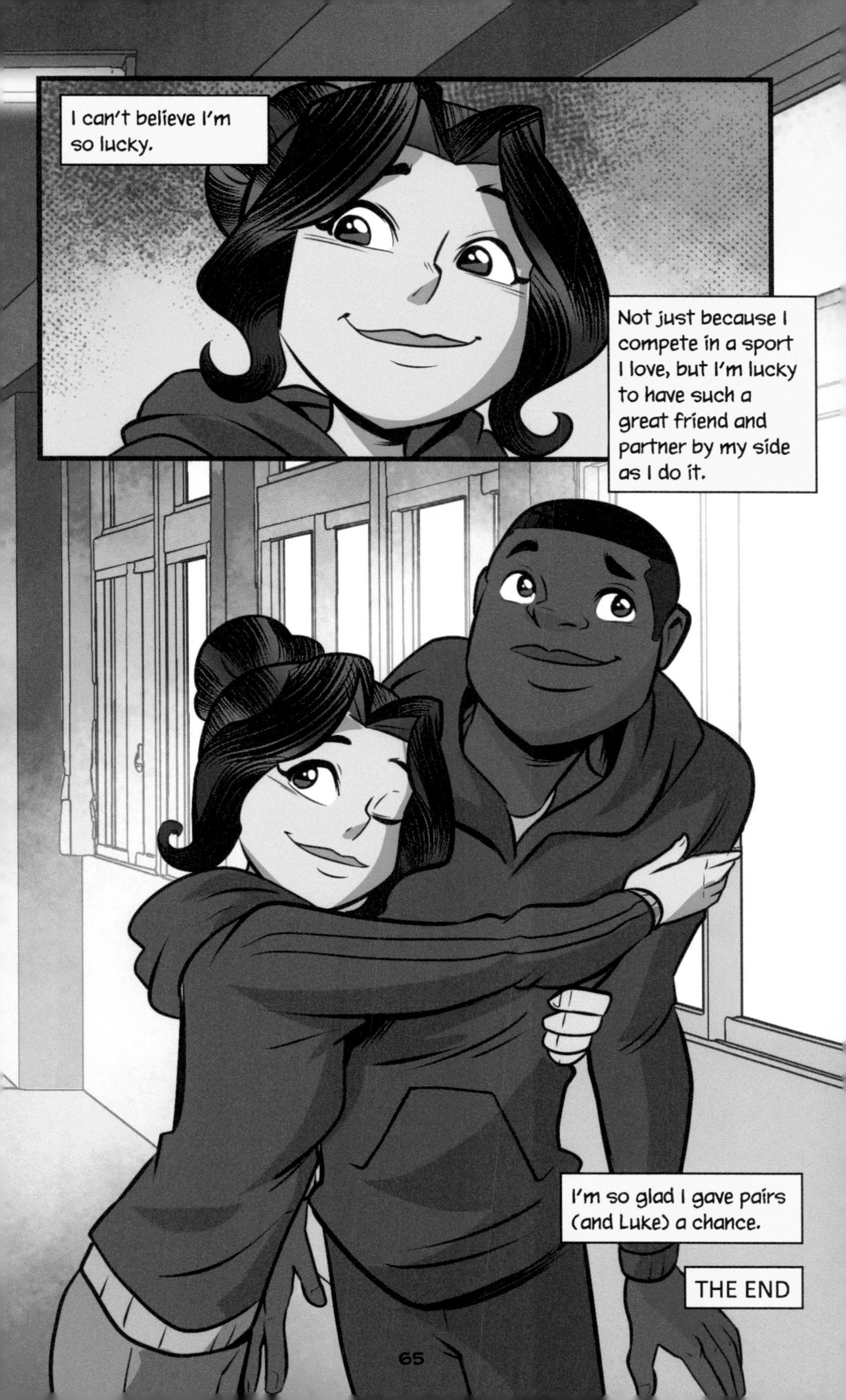
I can't believe I'm so lucky.
Not just because I compete in a sport I love, but I'm lucky to have such a great friend and partner by my side as I do it.
I'm so glad I gave pairs (and Luke) a chance.
THE END

VISUAL DISCUSSION QUESTIONS

1. Graphic novels combine words and pictures, but certain artistic effects can show movement too. Can you tell Mina is spinning in this image? How?

Pairs skating is, like, the most beautiful skating there is!

2. Artistic effects can also be a fun way to show emotions. Why do you think Mina's eyes are drawn as stars here? What do you think she is feeling?

3. Mina and Luke became more comfortable with each other the more they got to know each other. What hints does the art give to show that their skating improved because of it from the beginning of the story to the end?

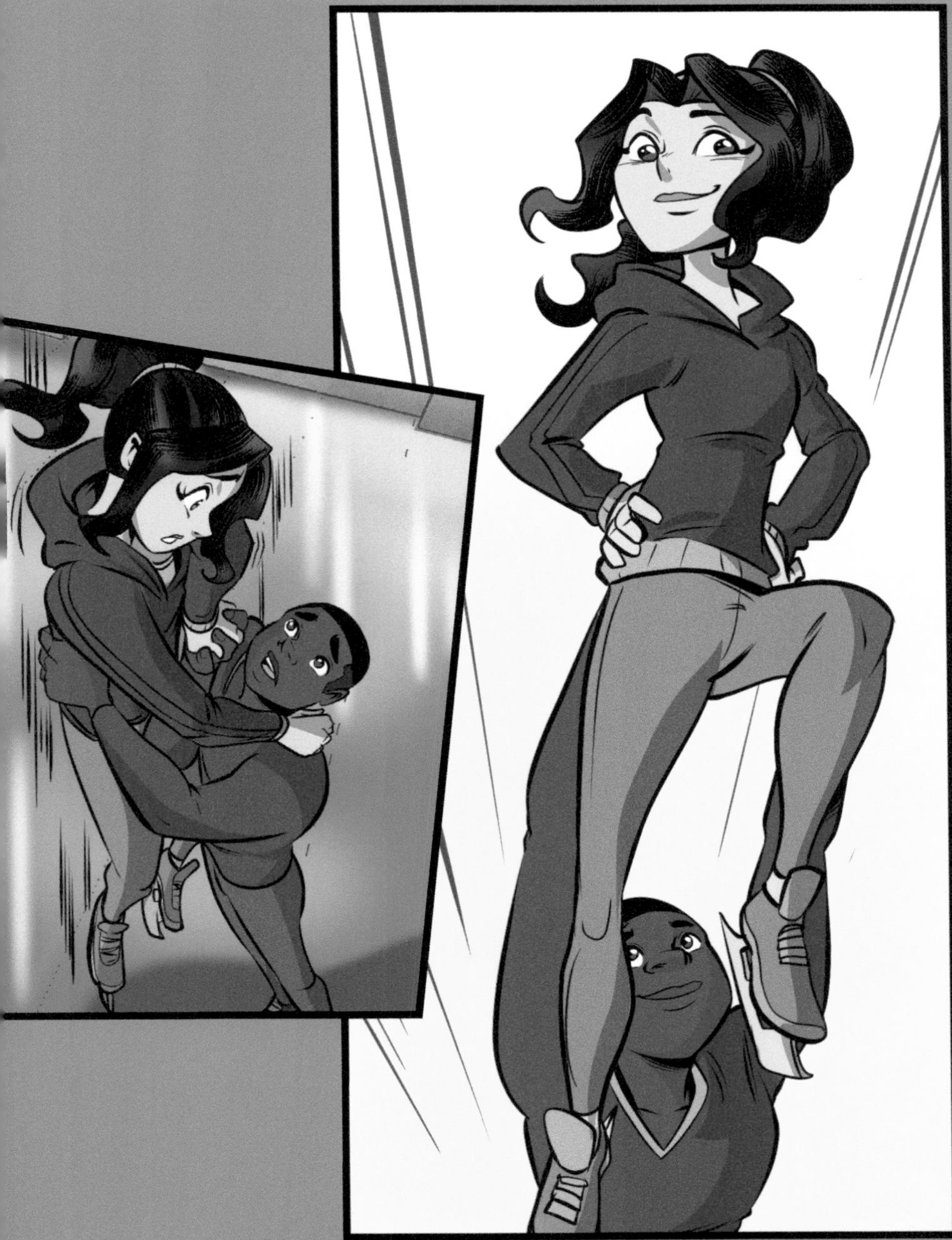

LEARN MORE ABOUT FIGURE SKATING

Skating on ice is an ancient tradition developed in Scandinavia as far back as 3000 BCE. The blades of the skates were made from animal bones. Iron blades weren't invented until the 1200s CE.

Well before trains or cars took over transportation, skates and sleds allowed for communication and supply runs between Scandinavian villages during the brutal winter months.

Skating for fun was one of the most popular hobbies throughout 1700s in Europe. Skate clubs were formed and even royalty such as Marie Antoinette enjoyed the pastime.

Recreational skating didn't used to be so graceful. That was changed forever in 1850 when Edward Bushnell designed the first steel blades that clipped into place. Skaters now had much more control on the ice, allowing for sharper turns and more complicated moves.

Olympic figure skating actually predates the Winter Games themselves! Figure skating was introduced in the 1908 London Olympic Games, while the first Winter Olympics wouldn't be until 1924.

Figure skaters can achieve amazing speeds! For instance, spins reach more than 300 revolutions per minute (RPM).

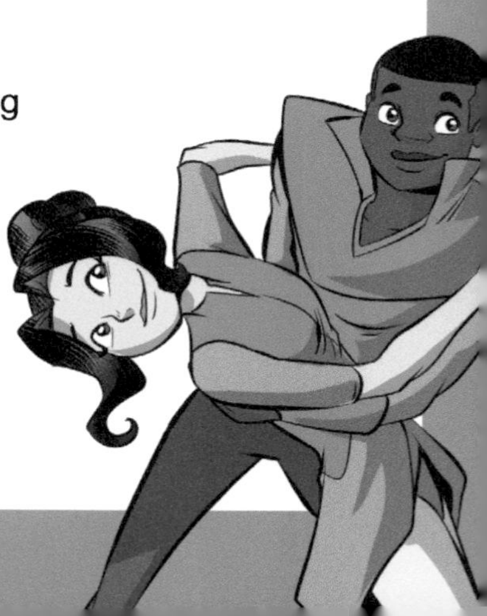

FAMOUS PEOPLE IN FIGURE SKATING

Jackson Haines

Jackson Haines was a successful ballet dancer in the 1800s. Bored by the basic skating moves of the time, Haines began performing spins, jumps, and other moves inspired by his dance background. He also skated to music, which was new. While seen as controversial in his lifetime, Haines is considered the founding father of modern figure skating.

Dr. Debi Thomas

In the 1980s, Debi Thomas became the first African-American woman to win the women's title at the U.S. Figure Skating Championships. She also won the World Championship. In 1988, she became the first African-American athlete to medal at the Winter Olympics in any sport. Thomas became a doctor, helping other athletes with injuries.

Michelle Kwan

Michelle Kwan is one of the most beloved athletes in U.S. Skating. Besides medaling in the 1998 and 2002 Olympics, she won the U.S. Championship and World Championship many times. After retiring from the sport, Kwan earned a graduate degree in international relations and later become an advisor for the U.S. State Department.

 GLOSSARY

anxious (ANGK-shuhss)—being worried

axel (AK-suhl)—a jump in which the skater skates forward, turns one and a half times or more in the air, and then lands and skates backward

complement (KOM-pluh-muhnt)—to go or work well with something or someone

core (KOR)—muscles that control the lower back and tummy

Lutz (LUTS)—a jump in which a skater glides backward in a wide curve and uses her toe pick to launch and rotate in the opposite direction

optimistic (op-tuh-MIS-tik)—expecting everything to come out all right

precise (pri-SISSE)—very accurate or exact

routine (roo-TEEN)—a series of tricks linked one after another in a performance on one apparatus

stability (stuh-BIL-uh-tee)—the quality of being firm and steady

ABOUT THE AUTHOR

Katie Schenkel is a comic writer best known for the critically acclaimed, Eisner Award-nominated graphic novel *The Cardboard Kingdom*. She especially loves to write about girls' friendships and their perspectives on the world around them. Her other books in the Jake Maddox series include *Basketball Camp Champ* and *Swim Team Trouble*. Midwest to her core, Katie lives in Chicago with her partner, Madison.

ABOUT THE ARTIST

Lelo Alves was born in Patos, a small town in the state of Paraíba, Brazil. While he was a teenager, he moved to the city of João Pessoa. Since Lelo was small, he never stopped drawing. The influence of alternative comics was his source of inspiration to enter in the field, with the support of friends and the help of co-workers.

Currently Lelo has works published in Brazil, Portugal, and the United States. He also works as an illustrator of children's books and game designer, as well as graphic design, which is his academic background.

READ THEM ALL!

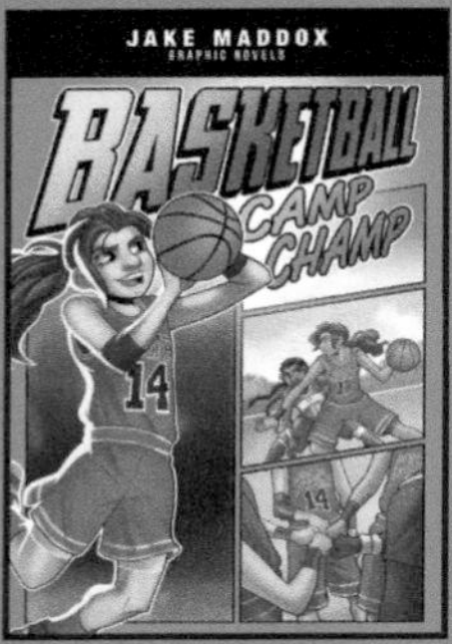
JAKE MADDOX
GRAPHIC NOVELS
BASKETBALL CAMP CHAMP

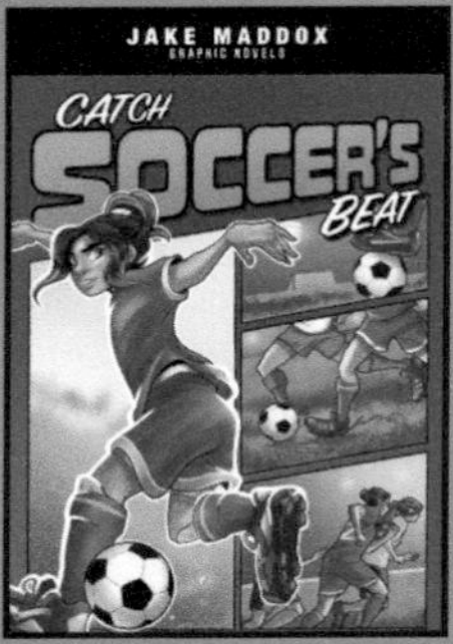
JAKE MADDOX
GRAPHIC NOVELS
CATCH SOCCER'S BEAT

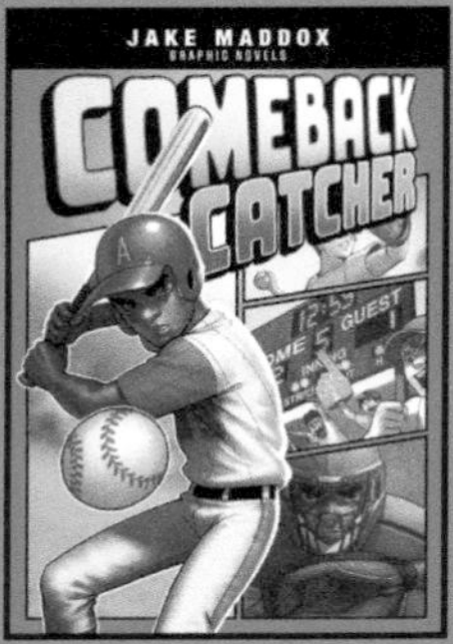
JAKE MADDOX
GRAPHIC NOVELS
COMEBACK CATCHER

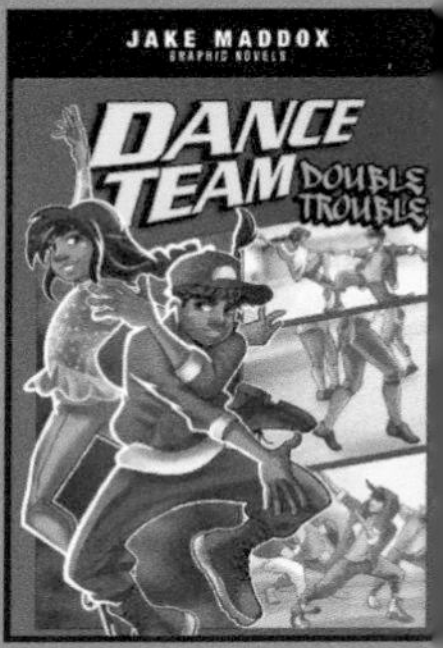
JAKE MADDOX
GRAPHIC NOVELS
DANCE TEAM DOUBLE TROUBLE

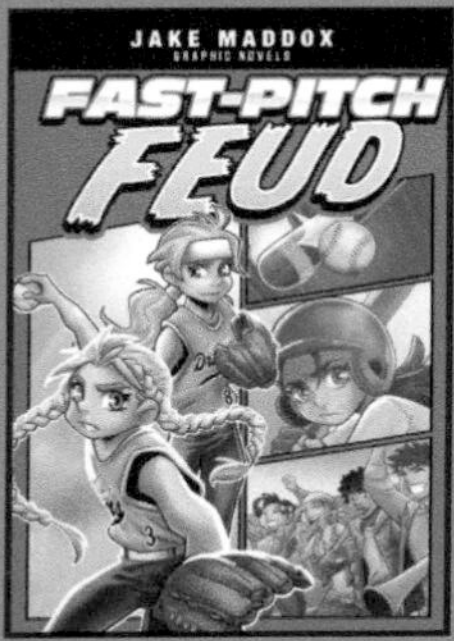
JAKE MADDOX
GRAPHIC NOVELS
FAST-PITCH FEUD

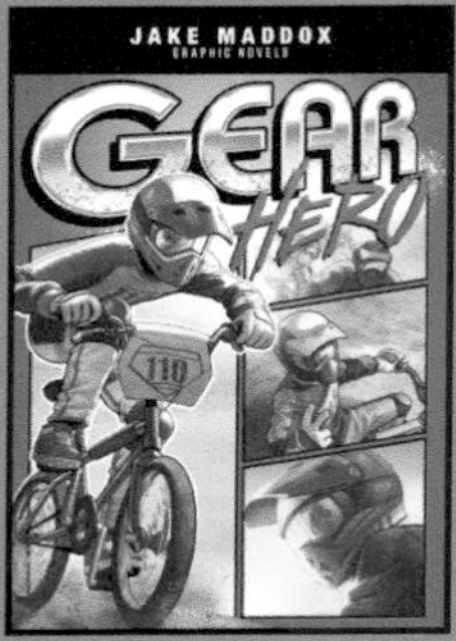
JAKE MADDOX
GRAPHIC NOVELS
GEAR HERO

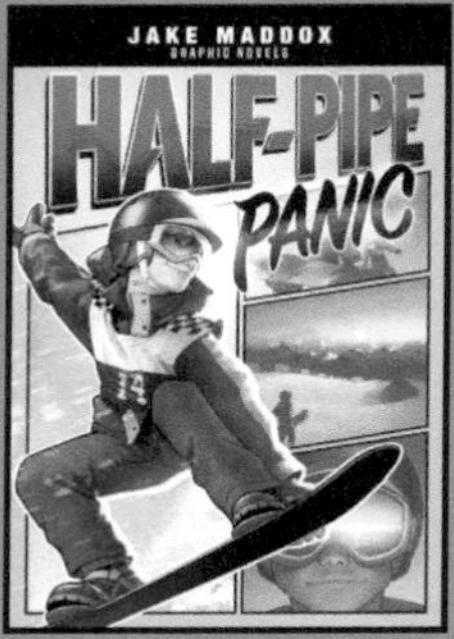
JAKE MADDOX
GRAPHIC NOVELS
HALF-PIPE PANIC

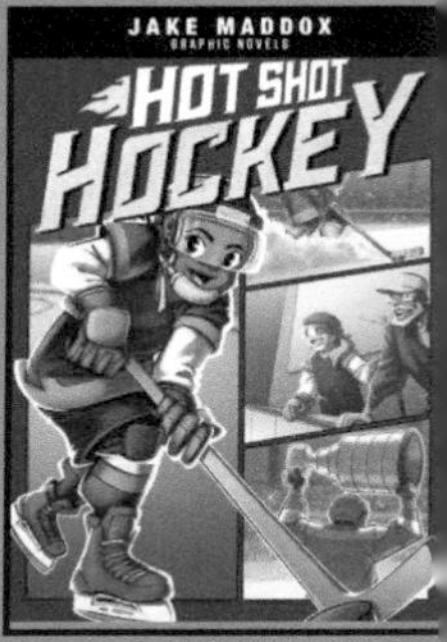
JAKE MADDOX
GRAPHIC NOVELS
HOT SHOT HOCKEY

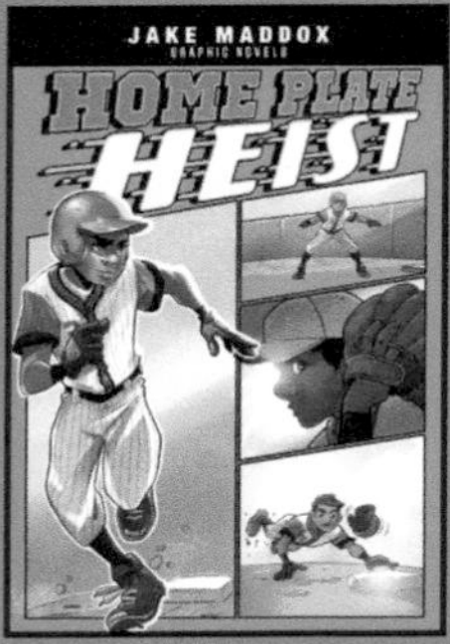
JAKE MADDOX
GRAPHIC NOVELS
HOME PLATE HEIST

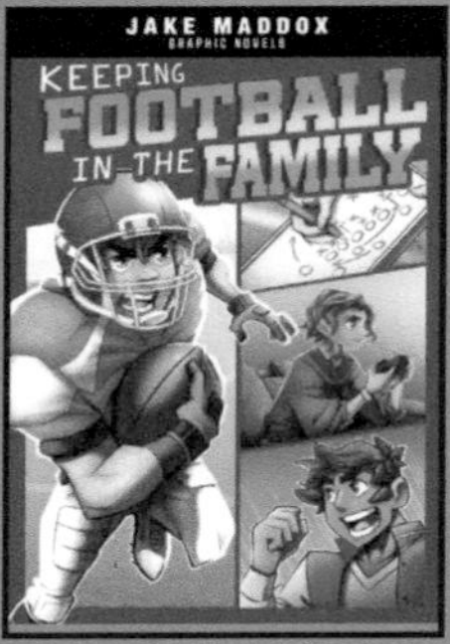
JAKE MADDOX
GRAPHIC NOVELS
KEEPING FOOTBALL IN THE FAMILY

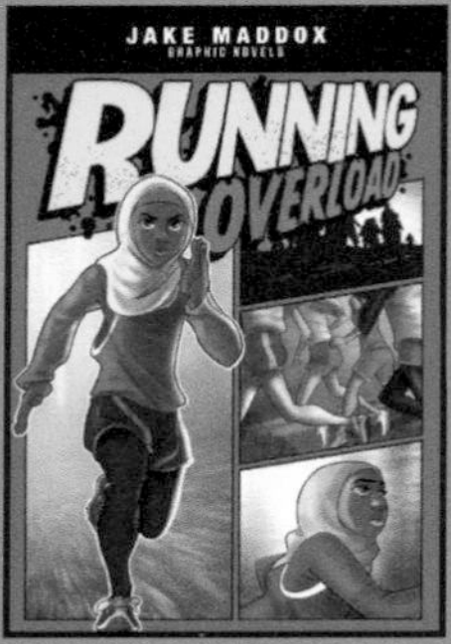
JAKE MADDOX
GRAPHIC NOVELS
RUNNING OVERLOAD

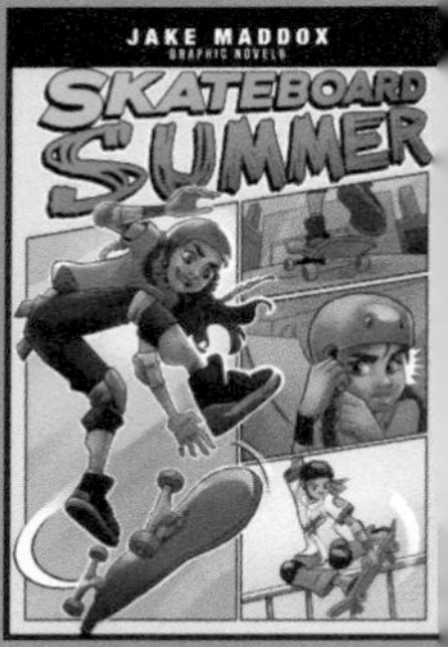
JAKE MADDOX
GRAPHIC NOVELS
SKATEBOARD SUMMER

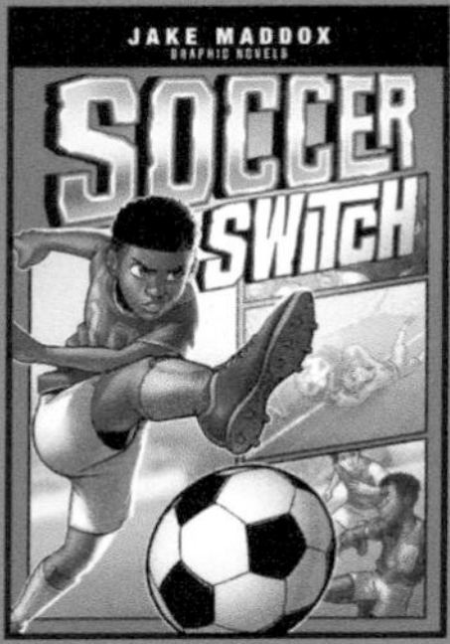
JAKE MADDOX
GRAPHIC NOVELS
SOCCER SWITCH

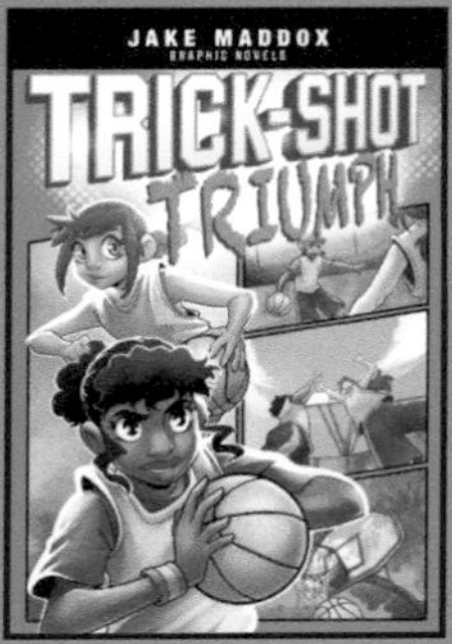
JAKE MADDOX
GRAPHIC NOVELS
TRICK-SHOT TRIUMPH

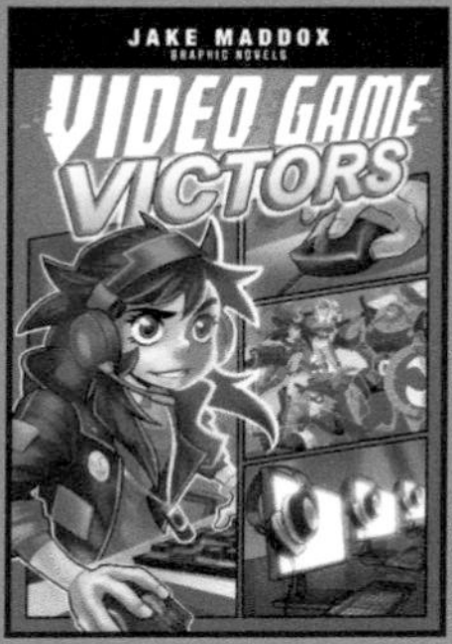
JAKE MADDOX
GRAPHIC NOVELS
VIDEO GAME VICTORS

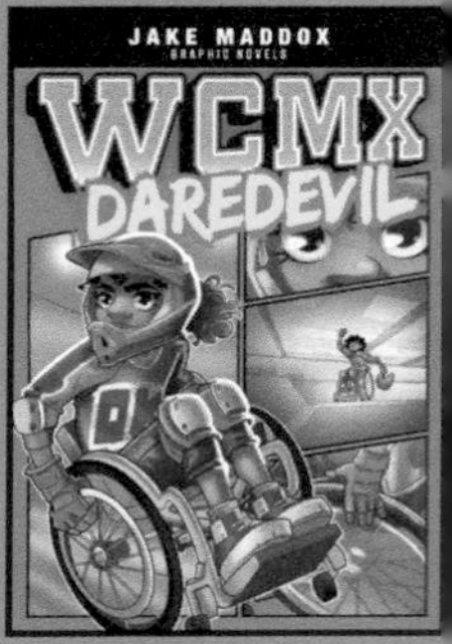
JAKE MADDOX
GRAPHIC NOVELS
WCMX DAREDEVIL